Primal Pleasure

Look for these titles by *Sydney Somers*

Now Available:

Pendragon Gargoyles
Primal Hunger
Primal Attraction
Primal Pleasure

Shadow Destroyers
Unbreakable
Stripped Away
Storm Warning
Dark Obsession

Spellbound
Say You're Mine
Don't Let Go
Whatever It Takes

Enslaved
Waitin' on a Hero
Call Me Cupid
Talons: Caged Desire
Trust Me

Print Anthology
Talons
Night Spell
Primal Seduction

Primal Pleasure

Sydney Somers

SAMHAIN
PUBLISHING

Samhain Publishing, Ltd.
11821 Mason Montgomery Rd., 4B
Cincinnati, OH 45249
www.samhainpublishing.com

Primal Pleasure

Print ISBN: 978-1-60928-299-8
Digital ISBN: 978-1-60928-147-2

Editing by Lindsey Faber
Cover by Kanaxa

First Samhain Publishing, Ltd. electronic publication: August 2010
First Samhain Publishing, Ltd. print publication: August 2011

Dedication

To the incredible Lindsey Faber. I'd be lost without you. This one makes ten books we've worked on together, and I can't wait for eleven and twelve and thirteen...

Chapter One

It was official—she was going to die shackled to a damn gargoyle.

Emma, twenty-third generation daughter of the House of Lamorak, let her hand fall back into her lap. The sound of the links clinking on the chain clasped around her right wrist only made the pain in her stomach worse.

If she'd been human, she would have sworn that being repeatedly dragged into her twin sister's escapades was giving her an ulcer. A two hundred-year-old ulcer, since that was how long she'd been roped into fixing Elena's problems.

She hadn't given up hope that one of these days her sister would learn to steer clear of trouble, or find a way to solve her messes on her own. At least, she hadn't given up hope until she'd found herself sporting the latest in magic-nulling accessories.

Emma eyed the silver and gold cuff she'd been stuck with for the last three days, no longer bothering to try getting free. The damn thing wouldn't budge. Neither would the other end that had been secured to the feral looking stone cat she leaned her back against.

For the hundredth time since she'd been left on the roof for refusing to undo a curse she hadn't cast, her attention drifted to the lackluster view of treetops and distant city skyscrapers.

Was it too much to ask that Elena piss off someone who favored penthouses and room service? Although, her current surroundings were quite a step up from the Korrigan's dungeon she'd spent a week in a few years back.

Thankfully, she didn't have to worry about the gargoyle breaking free of the stone at sunset and taking a chunk out of her. And judging by the size of the teeth permanently frozen in a menacing snarl, it would be one hell of a chunk.

She rarely crossed paths with gargoyles in their animal form, but guessed this one was bigger than most. Although she was seated on the ground next to it, the top of her head was still a few inches shy of the cat's back.

Not having to deal with the shifter's animal half was probably the only thing she had going for her given the enraged look on the gargoyle's face, one paw poised to slash something—or someone—to pieces.

While the threatening stance fit the reputation of a former member of the Guard—King Arthur's gargoyle protectors—it was at complete odds with everything else she'd learned about Cian Callaghan. Seeing as she hadn't been able to touch anything in his room below without being assailed by the memories connected to each object, she'd learned a lot.

Too much.

Nothing about the loyal, playful and charmingly arrogant man she'd glimpsed through those memories seemed to warrant the kind of punishment Elena had dealt him. It wouldn't be the first time her sister had overreacted and would doubtfully be the last—one of the drawbacks of such a fledgling sorceress channeling that much power.

Sighing, Emma shifted her weight and closed her eyes, soaking in the last of the setting sun's rays. How long until her captors realized that nothing she did would break the curse that had permanently locked the gargoyle in his stone form?

Only Elena could undo that, and since her twin had pulled another vanishing act, Emma was on her own. Of course, she could have just told her captors that they'd snatched the wrong sister—assuming they would have believed her.

God, how many times would she get stuck with the crap end of the stick before she let Elena dig her own way out of trouble? Problem-solving just shouldn't be that complicated for such an incredibly gifted sorceress.

At the very least, her sister deserved to cool her heels chained to a roof for a while. Too bad Emma couldn't hold on to that thought, knowing how heavily her twin relied on her magic.

One jerk on her chain reminded her of how powerless Elena would be against a furious gargoyle if forced to undo the curse she'd cast over a century ago. As much as she wanted to strangle her sister for inviting trouble, she'd do anything to protect her.

At least she had already left Leah, their human friend, when she'd realized the gargoyle's family was tracking her. Keeping Elena out of harm's way was enough of a challenge without worrying about Leah being caught up in everything along with her.

Sighing, Emma tugged on the cuffs of her long jacket, taking some small measure of comfort in the familiar weight of the leather. Even when the sun had been at its peak, she hadn't taken it off. Not only would she have felt naked and exposed without it, one look at her tracings—or lack thereof—and her captors would have realized she didn't possess enough magic to curse a three-day-old kitten, let alone a predator like the one she was chained to.

Out of habit she ran her fingers across the purple ivy markings encircling her wrist. Elena had over a dozen tracings—some she masked with magic—proof of her strength as a sorceress. Emma had three.

Recognizing the familiar invitation to a pity-party for one—the one event she'd sworn she'd outgrown decades ago—she tipped her face up.

"Could be worse," she mused, running her hand across the gargoyle's chest, imagining his heart was somewhere beneath her palm. "I could be trapped like you."

A soft rumble echoed on the air, and she straightened. She scanned the rooftop, but nothing moved except the late evening breeze stirring the few tendrils of hair that had escaped her braid.

Weird.

She settled back against the gargoyle, resigning herself to spending the night on the roof.

Warmth seeped into her back.

Frowning, she peered up at the cat. Until a few moments ago, she'd been hesitant to touch the gargoyle, but now curiosity pulled at her. She moved to her knees and ran a hand down his side.

Her gaze snapped to the gargoyle's face. Was he getting warmer?

Standing, she smoothed both hands down his sides, slowly returning to his face. Stone eyes stared back at her.

Of course nothing was happening. She hadn't cursed him and didn't have the kind of power to free him. That would have been too easy, for the both of them.

She dropped her head to the cat's. "Guess we're stuck with each other a while longer, huh?"

She refused to think about just how long they would leave her up here. Days. Weeks. Maybe even years if his family refused to accept that she couldn't undo the curse. The odds were higher that Elena might eventually notice she'd disappeared and come looking for her.

That could be days, weeks, or even years too.

"We're both so screwed."

The sound of something cracking had her head snapping up. She swung around, seeking the source, only to swivel back to the gargoyle. It took a minute to see the faint hairline cracks in the stone—cracks growing brighter. Brighter.

Holy shit.

Scrambling backward, she tripped over her own feet. The chain went taut before she had anything close to a reasonable space between them.

Bright light exploded outward, and she ducked, shielding her head. Immortal or not, even she couldn't survive decapitation. That, along with fire, was the only way to guarantee an immortal's death.

Emma braced for the debris that didn't come. The chain went slack, clattering on the roof, but she didn't move. Not until she felt the gargoyle's gaze burning into her. Hating the thought of being attacked while her back was turned, she lifted her head, determined to face the threat.

A warm breath puffed across the back of her neck.

Every cell in her body went still, anticipating the feel of the cat's teeth sinking into her flesh. Opening her palm, she prepared to at least try and defend herself with fire, only to remember the chain prevented it.

Not that the cat would have given her the chance anyway. One monstrous paw came into view beside her knee and then she felt the warm, wet swipe of his tongue.

Did he just...lick her?

She pivoted on her knees to face the cat just as he butted his head against her shoulder, knocking her on her butt.

Even though she knew the gargoyle had broken free, the sight of the large black feline staring at her with such vivid blue eyes froze her in place. She'd been this close to a dragon once when it had broken free of its stone—also thanks to Elena—but hadn't hung around long enough to get face-to-face.

A little in awe, she still had the sense to inch backward. It took another few seconds to realize she had enough slack to keep retreating. Without taking her eyes off the gargoyle, she drew the chain closer.

The other end was no longer attached to him.

Hope flared in her chest. So what if she didn't have a clue how to get away from the cat without him pouncing on her? She preferred to take it as a good sign that he didn't seem immediately interested in using her arm for a scratching post.

The cat rubbed his glossy black fur against her cheek, and she closed her eyes, indulging in the almost affectionate gesture. Growing up in Avalon, she'd never had a pet snuggle up against her. Even animals in the human world were wary of her, as if they all knew she'd once accidentally lit a friend's tail on fire when they were children.

Not the cat, though. The rumbling coming from his chest deepened, and she smiled. Only when she caught herself sinking her fingers into his thick coat, getting closer, did she realize her opportunity for escape was passing her by.

Regretful, she eased to her feet.

The cat instantly curled around her like a favorite tree he wanted to rub up against.

She took another step back, hesitating when she felt a shudder run through him. His paws seemed to tremble under his own weight and he swayed against her.

"What's wrong?" She nearly bent down, but her sense of self-preservation kicked in.

Run. Now.

Seeing the other end of her chain lying unhampered a few feet away, she wrapped as much of it as she could around her hand.

The cat growled in distress, collapsing next to her.

Go.

She backed away but didn't get more than a few steps before those blue eyes of his stopped her in her tracks. He needed her.

Don't be a fool. She could practically hear Elena in her head, demanding she look out for her own ass.

"I'm sorry."

A shower of bright-colored sparks rained over the cat, and she watched, dumbstruck, as he shifted from cat to man right before her eyes.

A naked man.

Her gaze slid over him, lingering on his broad shoulders before moving over the red dragon tattoo on his back and down to his—

"Wait." The raw whisper raced over her skin, speeding up her heart.

On his knees, the gargoyle struggled to raise his head. "Don't go."

She might have left without another word if he didn't look as though it would be the worst kind of betrayal. Making that feeling a hundred times worse were his eyes. They shouldn't be as intense on the man as they had been on the cat, and they damn well shouldn't make her feel as though he saw her.

Saw more than the responsible twin always bailing her

sister out of trouble. Saw more than the disappointing daughter her father had given up on long ago.

She shook her head. "I can't stay. If they come, I don't know what they'll do to me." The gargoyle might be free—and there would be time later to figure out how that had happened—but she doubted his family was going to thank her and send her on her merry little way. "I'm sorry."

"Please."

She closed her eyes at the sound of the rough plea. She'd made a mistake letting her curiosity get the better of her. If she hadn't deliberately touched the things in his room, wanting to know more about the gargoyle trapped in stone, it wouldn't be so hard to turn her back on him.

His chin dropped to his chest, his body shuddering.

Uncertain, she glanced around. Searching for an escape route or help? Damn it, she should never have touched his things. Why couldn't the chain have muted the gift she'd inherited from her Fae mother as well?

"Stay...please."

Hoping the delay wouldn't come back to bite her in the ass, she crouched next to him. She'd stay a minute, two tops, and then she'd go.

"Hey." She touched his shoulder, and they both hissed out a breath. His skin was freezing.

She stripped out of her jacket, sliding it down the chain until it draped over him, then rubbed with her hands to help warm him.

He kept his head down, his body shaking violently.

"You'll be okay soon," she murmured, hopeful. There was no way to know what kind of magical fallout might accompany a curse that had held for a hundred years.

"So...c-cold."

The tightness in her chest increased. Going to his family would definitely put a stop to any escape attempt, but she couldn't do nothing. He'd suffered enough thanks to her sister.

Sinking to her knees, she wrapped her arms around him, tucking her face against his neck.

He growled, and she jerked back. Had she hurt him?

One solid arm immediately swept her back in. "Closer." He rolled to his side, taking her with him, his unbreakable grip pinning her in place.

For ten seconds she didn't move. Didn't talk. Didn't squirm. Didn't breathe.

And apparently she'd had the right idea because the second she dragged in a quick breath, his tempting masculine scent came with it. Instantly, she remembered that it had been a while since she'd been this close to a man.

A naked man.

Okay, so she was a little preoccupied with the naked part. She could think about what that said about her when the gargoyle wasn't trembling all over.

Noticing just how naked he was might have only been a blip on her radar if he'd been primed to attack her. Except neither cat nor man had done more than rub against her. Even now, his body quaking, the gargoyle moved his hand across her back in shaky circles.

That had to explain why she found herself relaxing into him, settling her palm on his chest. Another rumbling growl echoed inside him, but before she could pull her hand back, he flattened it with his. This time when the same rough sound came, he nuzzled her cheek.

She sucked in a shocked breath, releasing it in slow

degrees as though it might stop her from wanting him to do it again.

It didn't work. And it really didn't stop her from turning her face toward his, feeling his rough jaw sweep across hers. She'd had her share of lovers, yet couldn't remember any of them ever holding her so possessively.

Her two minutes stretched into ten, maybe longer as his shaking slowly subsided to the occasional shiver. Good news if she didn't count the way his hands moved up her back, lulling her into melting against him.

Lulling her into some kind of false security for all she knew. Maybe that was how he planned to get even with her—lower her guard with lazy caresses and soft words.

Soft words?

She concentrated but couldn't understand what he whispered in her ear. Not that she cared when every warm breath and graze of his lips stirred something inside her.

Lust, she decided.

He was still naked, after all. Now that he wasn't trembling so badly, she didn't feel the least bit guilty drinking in the solid span of his shoulders and corded biceps. A faint line ran down the middle of his defined abdomen, disappearing into the shadow where their bodies pressed together. Trim hips and long legs extended well past her own, putting him well over six feet, she guessed.

Her gaze traveled back up, following the column of his throat to his jaw. She inched her head back a few degrees, finding his mouth. A cocky grin caught the corner of his mouth—one she recognized from the memory flashes—as though he knew exactly how much women enjoyed looking at him.

Knew how much she enjoyed looking at him.

Oh boy.

In half a second flat she found herself on her back with the gargoyle looming over her. Raised on his elbows, he wedged a thigh between hers, giving her no room to squirm away without rubbing against him.

Squirming was definitely out. So was breathing. Again.

“Don’t go.” Stronger but still rusty, his voice made her stomach grow hot and tight.

Only when she realized he waited for confirmation did she manage a slow nod. “Okay.” She just couldn’t figure out which of them she was lying to, since she’d ceased listening to her common sense right around the time he’d wrapped his arms around her.

Still, he stared at her, waiting.

God, when had the air grown so dry? She licked her lips and swallowed anxiously. “I’ll stay.”

Big mistake.

A lazy grin stole across the gargoyle’s face, as though she’d just offered herself up on a platter, slathered in whip cream.

Definitely a mistake. Too bad it was hard to remember that part when he dipped his head and nuzzled her throat.

Butterflies, the hot and silky kind, fluttered like mad under her ribs. She bit her lip only to have her breath hiss out as he trailed up to her jaw.

“I knew I’d find you.” He dragged his cheek across hers.

“We’ve never met.” She would have remembered the way his dark hair fell in careless strands across his forehead, or the arrogant slant to those full lips, as if he anticipated her complete surrender.

And there was no way she would have forgotten those eyes, especially when they turned almost feline on her.

"No, we haven't met." He teased his mouth along the sensitive skin below her ear. "But I've been waiting for you."

She shook her head, unsure which one of them was confused. It was damn hard to think clearly with his mouth setting fire to her insides.

He shifted his weight, settling tighter between her thighs. Pleasure shot through her, and it was all she could do to keep from betraying what he was doing to her. She didn't need her sister to tell her that kind of knowledge would give the gargoyle the upper hand.

Of course, if he kept sliding his thumb along the side of her breast like that, he could do whatever he wanted with his hands as long as he didn't stop.

Wonderful. Not only was she a poor excuse for a sorceress, she was as discriminating as an enchantress. It was well known the Lady of the Lake's daughters weren't that particular when it came to choosing bedmates.

Emma wasn't so different it seemed. She'd exchanged a handful of words with the gargoyle at most and made no effort to stop him from touching her. The opposite actually—she arched beneath him, biting her lip when his hand slid across her belly and edged beneath her halter-top.

"Your name," he pleaded, his nose bumping hers. "Tell me."

"Emma." She gripped his shoulders, felt his mouth slide closer. "My name is Emma." She trembled all over, squeezing her legs to satisfy the delicious ache the gargoyle had unleashed inside her.

He groaned against her cheek, and she felt his hand change course, sliding down between their bodies.

She whimpered and rolled her hips, craving the feel of his—

His head snapped up, tension turning his muscles into

sculpted rock. More animal than man, a menacing growl ripped from his throat. He planted one hand on the ground next to her, his eyes glittering with lethal intent.

"What it is?" The words had no sooner left her mouth than she heard the door to the roof bang open.

"Fuck me," someone said, probably one of the gargoyle's brothers. "She freed him." Retreating steps, then the voice yelled, "Cian's free."

Reality crashed in on Emma just as the gargoyle leaped over her. She scrambled up, her jaw dropping open as he shifted seamlessly into his cat form.

Instead of turning on her like she expected, he positioned himself between her and his brother Tristan. The one who was convinced he remembered Emma from the night her sister had cursed Cian.

She knew more about the Callaghans than they could imagine, which only made it that much harder to hate them for snatching her.

"Whoa!" Tristan held up his hands. "Easy, bro."

The cat didn't back off, his threatening snarl deepening when Tristan took a step toward him.

"Cian. Come on, man. Cool it." Tristan shot her a furious look when his brother didn't back off. "What the fuck did you do to him?"

"Nothing."

"Bullshit." He focused on the cat. "Come on, Cian. I'm not going to hurt you."

Seeming uncertain, the cat glanced back at her.

"Whatever you've done, fix it," Tristan snapped.

"I didn't do anything." Anything except screw up royally. She could have been gone. Even if it had meant dropping over the edge of the roof, she should have run when she had the chance. Any injuries, even the ones that hurt like hell, would have healed. A perk any immortal could appreciate.

And where Tristan was, the huntress who'd tracked and caught her couldn't be far behind. The sword the huntress wielded could most certainly do the kind of damage that could end an immortal's life, and Emma happened to like her head attached to her body, thank you very much.

When she had first realized the huntress was tracking her, she'd worried her sister had somehow exposed Avalon or the existence of immortals in the human realm. That was the only reason she could imagine the goddess Rhiannon would have dispatched a huntress.

Finding out that her sister had cursed the gargoyle—with one of Constantine's daggers no less—had made every one of Elena's past escapades pale in comparison. King Arthur's heir, Constantine, had crafted six mystical daggers that were rumored to reveal Excalibur's resting place, and countless immortals would kill to possess not only the daggers but also Arthur's sword.

The sword was prophesied to awaken Arthur so he could finish the war begun centuries ago, after he'd refused to satisfy his half-sister's thirst for power and make his nephew his heir. The war that had suffered a significant setback when he'd died fighting Morgana and his nephew Mordred at the battle of Camlann.

And Emma had been within reach of one of the daggers. The huntress had even removed the magic-nulling cuff from Emma's wrist, insisting she use the weapon to undo the curse. If she hadn't been so determined to convince them she couldn't help, she might have recognized the dagger instantly. Instead, she'd ignored it entirely.

Now she couldn't help but wonder how things would have turned out if she'd taken it. One touch and she might have been able to determine the location of another dagger, maybe all of them. That kind of knowledge would have been more than enough to bargain for her release, and yet she'd passed it up.

Passed it up like her recent opportunity for escape.

"Damn it," Tristan snapped, taking a threatening step in her direction, as though she had any control over the situation.

The cat instantly retaliated, driving him back.

"Why are you ready to tear my throat out? She's the one who locked you in stone for over a century."

Cold resignation sifted through her even as she felt the cat's attention move back to her.

Well, shit.

He was going to be sick, of that both cat and man were in perfect agreement. His vision swam and his stomach cramped, sabotaging the instinct to defend the female.

His female.

They wanted to hurt her. Didn't they?

He prowled the same path, every step making him more anxious and confused. Only when he edged closer to the female did the fuzzy veil clinging to his thoughts start to lift.

"Cian, look at me. We're brothers. You know me." The familiar voice didn't match the blur of shadows in front of him.

Why couldn't he see right?

"She did this to you, bro. Cursed you. You've been locked in stone since the night we went to that pub to celebrate." Tristan motioned toward the female, Emma. "She was there and I pissed her off..." He broke off, ran a hand through his hair.

Tristan. His brother.

Furious, Tristan stared at Emma. “Fix him.”

“I can’t.” The distress in her voice made him backtrack, and he rubbed against her.

She ran a hand through his fur though her gaze never left Tristan’s. More people stepped on to the roof and he growled, nudging Emma back.

“He’s protecting her.” The disgust in Tristan’s voice only agitated him more.

He recognized his sister’s scent before she said anything. “Cian?” Briana stopped beside Tristan.

“Don’t.” The female’s hand clamped down on the back of his neck before he could lunge at them. “They’re your family.”

She crouched down and he closed his eyes at the feel of her fingers sinking into his fur. He’d been waiting for her. Needed her.

“I don’t deserve your protection.”

Beneath the defeat in her voice, he felt her longing and ached to make it go away.

“It’s been a hundred years, Cian.” Briana stepped closer. “We haven’t seen you in over a century thanks to the sorceress you’re protecting.”

Still so cold, his thoughts foggy, he struggled to understand.

Emma’s hand fell away from him as she stood and took a step back. “They’re telling the truth.”

Chapter Two

"You haven't eaten enough."

Cian shrugged, not taking his eyes off the flat screen mounted on the wall in the kitchen. He'd eat later, use the glass and metal box on the counter to warm something up like Tristan had shown him, though he couldn't remember what it was called.

Food hadn't changed nearly as much as the rest of the world—except maybe fast food. The Big Mac was definitely a creation he'd enjoyed the hell out of a couple hours ago after seeing a human eating one on the screen.

A television, he mused again, still stunned by the countless changes he'd missed in the last hundred years. Anger surged inside him at the reminder, though he'd gotten better at forcing it back in the last two days.

"Hey." Briana touched his shoulder.

"I'm okay."

They both knew he was lying, but she didn't address it further. Time, she'd said. He just needed time to adjust to the changes in the human world. The hardest part wasn't that he'd lost a hundred years in the blink of an eye, but that he'd been so overwhelmed by it all he hadn't taken a step off the property yet.

He might have been tempted to follow Tristan's suggestion to return to Avalon if not for the sorceress cooling her heels in his suite of rooms.

Before his thoughts could drift to the black-haired temptress, he focused on the television. He wouldn't be able to put off seeking her out for much longer. The cat was riding him too damn hard, not caring what she'd done.

He hadn't cared either at first, his judgment clouded after spending so long trapped in stone. But his family had finally succeeded in getting through to him after he'd shifted back to his human form—barely. His animal half had fought the shift, determined to protect Emma.

Even now the cat prowled restlessly in the back of his mind, needing to be close to her, but not nearly as much as the man needed it. Thankfully, he literally had hundreds of distractions to keep him occupied. Every room in the mansion held objects he'd never seen before, capable of things he could barely imagine.

So why then did his thoughts always circle back to Emma?

He'd understand if he had vengeance on his mind. But whenever he started out thinking of a way to inflict a suitable punishment for the years she'd cost him, his thoughts always turned from punishment to pleasure.

Chaining her up in Avalon's catacombs and leaving her to rot for a hundred years ended up as chaining her to his bed. Handing her over to a Korrigan, knowing the lethal fairy would enthrall her into eternal servitude, ended with him imagining her catering to his every carnal whim.

Hell, even his brief notion of putting himself out of his misery and feeding her to one of the Forgotten—gargoyles that had permanently embraced their animal halves—had turned to devouring her himself, starting at her toes and licking his way up her body...

Sweet Avalon, someone needed to knock some sense into him.

"The sun is going to be up soon." Briana put away the food he'd ignored. It didn't appeal to him as much as another Big Mac. "You sure you're going to be fine on your own? I can call Tristan."

Somehow he managed not to roll his eyes. "I don't need anyone to mind me."

One slim brow arched upward, and he knew she was thinking about the havoc he'd wreaked in her rooms earlier.

Cian held up his hands. "I won't go near your wing of the house. I swear it."

Not even the lure of a Big Mac would make him venture anywhere near his sister's suite of rooms for a long time to come. He wasn't afraid to admit her computers and countless other gadgets scared the hell out of him.

The only time he'd gotten curious and poked around, he'd set off a dozen alarms. By the time Briana had darted out of the bathroom, her hair still wrapped in a towel from her shower, the cat inside him had broken free at the unfamiliar threat.

Apparently his sister was rather fond of the metal boxes he'd batted across the floor. She probably would have done more than kick him out of her room if he hadn't been gone for a century.

Remembering the look on her face when she surveyed the damage brought a smile to his face. Tristan and their oldest brother, Cale, had been inseparable when they were younger, leaving Briana at Cian's mercy when they were cubs.

He couldn't even begin to count the times and ways he'd tormented her in hopes of getting her riled up. Though with three older brothers, it hadn't taken her long to adapt and turn the tables on them.

After the incident with the sorceress, his family had vowed to stick together until he was freed. Now that they'd accomplished their goal, he wasn't sure how much longer they'd be living under one roof. Especially with both of his brothers mated now.

He hadn't realized he'd shared that last thought aloud until Briana laughed.

"Try not to sound so happy for them," she teased.

"I am happy for them." Finding a mate was the only thing that gave a gargoyle control over the automatic shift to stone at sunrise.

The goddess Rhiannon had punished all gargoyles—cats, wolves and dragons—for King Arthur's death, blaming them for failing to protect him. Rhiannon hadn't cared that her son was prophesied to awaken when Excalibur was returned to him, and condemned the gargoyle clans to spend their daylight hours trapped in their stone form.

Rhiannon might eventually have gotten past her grief long enough to lift her punishment if Arthur's enemy hadn't claimed Camelot. Morgana continuing to rule the heart of Avalon was just one more reason for Cian to stay in the human world, as far as he was concerned.

"So," Briana began. "There's more food in the fridge. If you want to stretch out, there's the T.V. in the den. You remember how to work the remote?"

He didn't have a clue what the remote was, but nodded anyway. Otherwise she'd want to show him again, which would then lead to another explanation about something else and then another.

Truthfully, he'd started looking forward to sunrise an hour

ago. As much as he loved his sister and how much she was trying to help, she talked—a lot. Not only did he need a break from processing everything, the headache he hadn't been able to shake since breaking free of the stone was starting to make him nauseous.

Maybe another Big Mac would help.

"The number for Pendragon's is on the counter and programmed into the phone I gave you," Briana continued. "Tristan will be there most of today and tonight since Cale is still in Avalon with Sorcha."

Cian wasn't sure what surprised him most. That his family owned a bar that catered to both humans and immortals, or that Cale was mated to a huntress. He still shuddered over the latter even though Sorcha wasn't as scary as he'd imagined. Her sword was, though.

Briana leaned against the counter. "You do have your phone on you, right?"

If she was referring to the compact device he'd been carrying around in his pocket until it started shaking like some kind of explosive he'd seen on television, then no. But if he admitted that she'd make him go get it, and he'd be damned if he got lost in concentration only to have that thing take him by surprise again.

She gave him a quick squeeze. "You should try to get some sleep."

"Or not." Even if he were tired, he wouldn't have been able to sleep more than a few minutes at a time. Part of him worried if he fell asleep for too long, he'd find another hundred years had passed him by.

"Well, don't go too far."

"I may be reckless upon occasion, but I'm not stupid, Briana."

"I just meant that we don't know how long you'll be immune to the sun after being imprisoned, so it's best not to go exploring—"she glanced pointedly at the fast food bag on the table next to him, "—and turn to stone in the middle of an intersection somewhere."

They'd all been surprised when he hadn't gone to stone during the first sunrise after the sorceress had freed him. A temporary perk, though Emma had refused to say how long it would last.

He planted a quick kiss on Briana's forehead. "I'll be fine. Truly," he added when she didn't budge. "You're going to end up blocking the doorway if you turn down here, you know."

She sighed, and after one last look he swore was meant to remind him not to treat her stuff like oversize balls of yarn, she left.

Cian stayed in the kitchen another couple of hours, eventually digging out half the food that Briana had left behind. Stacks of newspapers and magazines Tristan had found him littered the tabletop and half the counter by the time he finished snacking and rifling through it all.

Leaving the kitchen, he started for the den, only to backtrack when he passed the hall leading to his rooms. Being with Emma on the roof, however briefly, had burned her scent into his brain. Nowhere in the mansion offered him enough distance to escape the lure of it.

Now, knowing she was only a few doors away...

Determined, he continued on. He made it another six steps, then stopped.

Had Briana brought her any food tonight? As angry as he was for what Emma had done to him, the idea of her going hungry didn't sit well.

Before he could remind himself that Briana wasn't as

thoughtless as the sorceress, his animal half urged him down the hall. A quick check on her wouldn't hurt, or so he thought until every step he took made his heart thump faster.

It took another minute to realize it was anticipation and not anger that made his blood run hot through his veins. That should have been enough to stop him in his tracks. Instead he almost snapped the handle off as he shoved the door open.

A lamp had been left on in the main room—the empty main room.

Of course she couldn't have just been curled up on the leather couch. Right then he knew he should have listened to Tristan, who had insisted on putting Emma in the cellar. Maybe then he wouldn't be thinking about her snuggled under his covers.

Too easily he imagined tugging the blanket down, slowly exposing her bitable neck and all the soft, creamy skin he'd been thinking about since the roof.

Lust snaked down his backbone, settling heavy and hard behind his zipper.

He cursed under his breath but didn't try to curb the desire unleashed by the scent of her. He hadn't had a woman in over a century, and admitting an intense attraction to Emma wasn't the same as acting on it.

There would have to be something wrong with him if he didn't respond to her. Women, human or immortal, had been a favorite pastime, and as soon as he became accustomed to everything, he had every intention of seeking out a willing female to satisfy the need building inside him.

The cat snarled at the edge of his mind, but Cian ignored it, crossing to his bedroom and frowning into the darkness.

She wasn't in his bed.

He shook his head as though it would wipe away the carnal images of Emma arching beneath him, her nails raking his back, and listened.

The sound of running water registered first, then the thin slash of light that escaped the side of the bathroom door. Halfway across the room, he spotted the thin chain snaking across the floor and disappearing between the door and the frame.

Briana had anchored the other end of the chain in his room before giving him the key that was presently burning a hole in his pocket. By the time he reached the door, the flicker of disappointment at not finding her in his bed had vanished. A new hotter, hungrier tension rippled under his skin.

He tried the handle, surprised when the door moved easily. Either she hadn't been expecting him since he'd gone out of his way to avoid her, or she realized somehow barricading the door wouldn't be worth the effort.

Or maybe she wasn't even in the shower, water sliding down her body, beading off her nipples, waiting for him to catch the trailing drops with his tongue.

Cian squeezed his eyes shut, but the door gave way as though he couldn't stop it. Like a man possessed, he slipped into the room, intent on making sure she hadn't somehow escaped before he figured out what to do with her.

As if you don't already know.

Ignoring that thought before it could get him into trouble, he let his eyes adjust to the bright light. He noticed her clothes first—some in a pile on the floor while her shirt and jacket had been threaded through the chain next to it.

It took only a second to spot her through the frosted glass.

There, he'd seen that she hadn't found a way to slip away on him. He should go. The cat growled in protest, wanting to be close to Emma. The man wasn't exactly in disagreement, so he lingered another moment.

Steam clouded the air, the damp heat making him even hotter. She stayed so still he assumed she'd noticed him, then she slowly turned her face up to the spray.

He gripped the door handle tighter, prepared to leave—determined to—right up until she shook out her braid and all that long black hair. Entranced, he let his gaze follow the curling strands all the way down to the small of her back, then lower, cursing the frosted glass the whole way.

Taking another three steps into the room, he thought about sliding the door across to get a much better look at those enticing naked curves. The need only intensified when she reached for the soap. Already hard for her, he was aching by the time she slid the bar of soap over her hip and up to her breasts.

The sorceress was slaying him to pieces. Much more and she'd have to step over his body to get out of the bathroom.

"You're staring."

His gaze snapped to her face, and she glanced over her shoulder at him.

He shook his head. He stared at beautiful women or females with really incredible breasts. What he did now, his quick exit forgotten, wasn't so much staring as it was devouring.

She slid the door open a couple of inches. "Here to scrub my back, gargoyle?"

Her back wasn't a bad place to start. Then her hips perhaps, and that sweet curve leading down to the inside of her thighs...

Definitely slaying him.

"So if you're not staring and don't plan on scrubbing my

back, what are you doing in here?"

Cian waited until she rinsed her hair before answering. There wasn't much point in talking if her head was under running water, and if it gave him another moment to watch her through the glass, there was no harm in that either. "I wanted to see if you were hungry."

She shut off the water. "Is stale bread and water on the menu?"

"That's what my family has been feeding you?"

"No, but then they don't hate me as much as you do."

He would have nodded if not for the cat threatening to break free. The instinct to protect her, even from himself, left him uncomfortable in his own skin.

Annoyed with the present situation, one he'd put himself in the second he sought her out, he crossed his arms and leaned against the vanity.

Emma's brows crinkled together. "Towel, please."

He didn't move.

She slid the glass open another few inches, her face wet and flushed from the hot water. "They're right behind you." She pointed over his shoulder as though to redirect his gaze from her.

Now that he was paying attention, she didn't seem nearly at ease with him there as she let on. She shifted her weight, her breaths whispering unevenly past her lips. Despite that, she didn't break eye contact, seeming to sense that backing down in any way would give the predator in him the edge.

Suspecting she'd just brazen it out if he were enough of an ass to pass her a hand towel, he snagged the closest oversize one. Without the water beating down her scent, it wrapped around him until he couldn't take a breath without feeling like he was taking her in.

And it felt good. Too good for a woman who had robbed him of a hundred years.

Throwing the towel over the glass, he glared at her. "Hurry up."

"Or what, you'll come in here and get me? That is what you cats do, don't you? Strong-arm your females into doing everything you say?"

"You are *not* my female."

An unreadable emotion blinked across her face, then she smiled sweetly. "Thank the gods for that."

Emma took her time getting dressed and towel-drying her hair. She hadn't seen him since they'd come down from the roof, and his unexpected appearance had rattled her. Briana had warned her that Cian would decide what to do with her, and she'd been preparing herself for his anger, assuming she didn't find a way to escape first.

But anger hadn't been what she'd glimpsed on his face when she noticed him in the bathroom, not at first anyway. His expression had been much too...carnal.

She shivered despite the chain clinking against the vanity, reminding her of her precarious situation. She was familiar enough with the way men looked at women when they had sex on their minds to recognize it instantly.

Only Cian had taken it to another level entirely, like moving from the heat of a warming ray of sunshine to full-scale nuclear meltdown.

When her insides threatened to ignite all over again, she pulled the borrowed comb harder through her wet hair. She had enough to deal with without overanalyzing the last few minutes—like the six-foot-plus gargoyle pacing on the other side of the door.

Were all cats so high strung, or just the ones who had been locked in stone for a few decades?

Elena had really done it this time. Maybe if her sister stopped and overanalyzed things once in a while, Emma would be spared from dealing with the repercussions of her sister's impulsive actions.

Twice Cian pounded on the door for her to hurry up. Both times she ignored him. Rushing would mean acknowledging how much he intimidated her. Without strong magic to rely on, she'd learned early that most confrontations were avoidable as long as she didn't show any weakness.

Okay, there was a tiny, foolish part of her that wanted to see if he actually planned on dragging her out of there. Maybe if he got rough with her, she'd be able to stop thinking about the way he'd been staring at her earlier and when they'd been on the roof.

Telling herself he'd been confused and bewildered after the sudden change hadn't been working to erase the memories of his mouth brushing her cheek.

How was it that their near kiss did more for her than her last boyfriend had? And the Fae has been pretty talented with his mouth. She hadn't had any complaints at the time, or none she'd admitted to herself, until the jerk dumped her for a sorceress whose magic was both "potent and predictable". Asshole.

Another pound on the door was followed by a scraping sound.

His claws?

The sound should have made her retreat instead of edge closer to the door. Maybe if she wasn't thinking of him using a claw or two to strategically slice away her clothes.

God, she needed help. She studied her reflection. How long did Stockholm Syndrome usually take to kick in? Never mind that she'd spent most of her time alone, wondering what he planned to do with her.

Not wanting to appear as though she were hiding out, she finally strolled out of the bathroom—and right into a solid wall.

Two arms slipped around her, steadying her when she bounced backward.

"You took too long," he growled.

"Sorry. Didn't realize you kept your prisoners on such a tight schedule. What's next, time in the exercise yard? Or maybe laundry duty?"

"Better a prisoner than..." He abruptly released her without finishing.

"Dead? Is that what you were going to say?"

"And what do you think is a fitting punishment for what you did to me?"

The only punishment Emma had in mind was for her sister. "Time served?"

He snorted and motioned for her to follow him.

Wary, she hung back. "You're letting me leave the room?"

Without answering, he unlocked the chain from the bolt on the floor. She watched him pocket the key, not bothering to hide her interest. His lethal smile dared her to try and retrieve it.

She shrugged. "Maybe later."

In a blink he closed the distance between them, grabbing her hand.

Her gaze dropped to where his warm fingers encircled her

wrist. “Are you always hands-on with your prisoners?”

Releasing her instantly, he frowned. “No tricks.”

She jiggled her wrist, rattling the chain that nulled what little magic she did possess. “Only because you said please.”

Emma thought she glimpsed a smile on his lips before he preceded her out of the room. She fell into step with him, trying not to let her fear show. He could have been lying about feeding her for all she knew, wanting to keep her cooperative for as long as possible.

Suspicious, she watched him from the corner of her eye. He even moved like a predator, each step fluidly lethal, as though he could turn on a dime and have his teeth buried in her throat.

Like the others before, that thought wasn’t nearly as disturbing as it should have been. Was there a syndrome for imagining your captor had a thing for you? Suddenly that kind of condition seemed the more dangerous of the two.

Feeling her gaze on him, Cian glared at her.

“You cut your hair,” she offered, as it if it were a perfectly reasonable explanation for looking at him.

Seeming puzzled, he nodded, leading her into the spacious kitchen.

She lingered in the doorway a moment, feeling a stab of envy. She’d been tempted to update her own kitchen more than once only to be talked out of it every time. According to Elena, what was the point of a state-of-the-art kitchen if Emma would just blow things up in it?

Though maybe if she invested in a few cooking classes, she wouldn’t feel compelled to add a touch of magic to speed the culinary process along.

A slight jerk on the chain refocused her attention on Cian.

He turned away from the fridge, his hands loaded with plates of food, nodding for her to take a seat at the table.

It hadn't been that long since she'd eaten last but her stomach rumbled at the sight of the food. This time she was sure she didn't imagine the smile flicker across Cian's face. He set the plates down and turned to the laptop propped open on the counter.

Assuming he had no intention of eating with her, she plucked a cold piece of chicken from the closest plate and took a bite. Cian kept his back to her while she worked her way through two pieces of chicken and some cold pasta salad. His fingers tapped away at the keys, each stroke becoming more of a stab as he started to mutter to himself.

When he cursed for the third time, she gave in to her curiosity. "Problem?"

He didn't acknowledge that she'd said anything, but moved over a little, letting her see the screen.

She waited until he cursed again, his fingers hitting the keys so hard she wasn't sure which of the pair was going to come away unscathed, then joined him at the counter.

He shoved the laptop aside. "It's not working."

Glancing at the flashing cursor, she tugged the machine toward her, anticipating the memories that came with touching it. Most were tied to Briana, but the most recent were Cian's, and with only a few keystrokes she understood his mounting frustration with technology.

"What's the password? Come on," she added when he wasn't immediately forthcoming. "I'm a sorceress not a hacker."

His brows drew together. "Hacker?"

"Someone really good with computers."

He didn't look convinced.

"I shop online, gargoyle. I don't fleece people's bank accounts. Though I once dated a dragon that built himself quite a little nest egg in the Cayman Islands that way."

Cian growled and turned away.

Yeah, she hadn't approved of her date's questionable pastime either, but doubted the gargoyle cared about that. He'd already made up his mind about her.

"Pendragons," he finally admitted in a skeptical tone.

She typed in the password, and noticed Cian's I-told-you-so look when the box flashed and denied her access.

Ignoring him—until he stepped up behind her anyway—she frowned at the keys. "Caps lock is on." She retyped the password and gave him a triumphant smile when it unlocked and loaded the operating system. "Don't suppose we're even now?"

He leaned in, peering over her shoulder at the screen. "Just be sure to put the key to your chain under the mat when you leave."

Emma rolled her eyes. Wasn't he just hilarious?

Cian pointed to the Internet browser icon. "That one."

"Want to surf for a while, huh?"

"We're not near the ocean."

"What?" She glanced over her shoulder, saw the confusion on his face. "I meant surf the web. Sorry," she added when he finally nodded. Turning back to the laptop, she mumbled, "Must be a lot to adjust to."

She cringed as soon as the words left her mouth. She'd taken a page right out of Elena's speak-before-you-think book with that one. Instantly she felt his gaze boring holes into the back of her head. At least his claws stayed sheathed.

For now.

Cursing her sister for the thousandth time, she opened the web browser. "There you go. Just try not to go blind looking at porn," she added, hoping to break the tension a little.

"Porn?"

She took a step back, forgetting he was directly behind her, and froze. "As in pornography. Naked pictures of women. People having sex."

"And you've seen this?"

"It's hard to go many places on the net without coming across it at some point." She was about to slide to the right when he planted his arm on the counter, hemming her in. "I've seen some," she finally admitted, hoping the right answer would release the biceps barricade between her and the table.

"Show me."

Not caring how close they stood, her gaze darted to meet his. "What?"

"Show me," he repeated, the seductive edge to his voice making her blood push faster through her veins.

Chapter Three

He jiggled the other end of the chain. “Unless you would prefer to return to your cell?”

Tricky son of a bitch. She’d watch hippos have sex if it meant delaying her return to the same set of walls she’d been staring at for days.

“Whatever you say.”

“I do believe you’re starting to understand, sorceress.” His arrogance thankfully kept her body from overheating at his continued proximity.

Focusing every brain cell on the laptop, she did as he asked.

He, on the other hand, seemed oblivious to everything but her. “Why would I go blind?”

“Huh?” He was making it damn hard to concentrate when she knew his mouth all but brushed her ear when he spoke.

“You warned me not to go blind looking at porn.”

“I was joking. I didn’t mean watching people have sex would make you go blind. More like what you’d be doing while watching.” She stopped there, distracted by the sudden image that popped into her head.

“Yes?” he pressed.

Emma cleared her throat. “Human mothers used to say it

to their sons so they wouldn't, you know."

"No, I don't know."

He sounded truly baffled, but she wasn't about to search his face to determine whether or not he was screwing with her. She was distracted enough without another visual confirmation of how close he was to her mouth.

"Masturbate." She couldn't get the word out fast enough. She wasn't usually uncomfortable talking about sex, but thinking about the gargoyle wrapping his hand around his cock to pleasure himself...

"Anyway," she breathed. "There's lots of other stuff to check out on the Internet. Facebook maybe or Twitter. You Tube."

He shook his head, leaned closer. If she turned her face just a little to the left, his lips would be right there.

Damn it, what was wrong with her? If she didn't know Cian was a gargoyle, she'd be convinced he was a sorcerer just masking the extent of his tracings. Among her kind, power unconsciously drew others like a moth to a flame, and it would have at least helped explain her intense awareness of every move he made.

She'd been unconsciously drawn to a powerful sorcerer once, one she had no intentions of getting involved with—ever—but even that paled in comparison to what she was feeling right now.

"There you go." She slid the laptop down the counter when an adult website popped up, hoping he'd slide right along with it.

He reached around her and pushed it back. "Continue."

Only in a dream would it have been that easy, she supposed.

Thinking she'd strap him down and subject him to hours of

hippo sex if the tables were ever turned, she entered the site, mentally bracing herself for whatever images appeared.

Cian leaned in, his chest snug against her back now. God, he was throwing enough body heat to sink right through her leather jacket.

"So what's your poison? Standard guy-girl stuff? Oral sex? Girl-on-girl action?" She was almost hoping for the latter to help curb her rising temperature.

He pointed to an image on the screen of a guy going down on a woman.

O-kay then.

Emma scrolled the mouse over the photo and hit the enter key before glancing away. There was only so much she could take, and she was fast approaching that threshold no matter how hard she tried talking herself down.

"It makes you uncomfortable." No seductive tone this time, just truth.

Too bad she found his voice sexy as hell even when he wasn't trying to use it against her.

Soft moans drifted from the laptop speakers as the video she'd clicked on began to play.

She wet her dry lips, studied the counter. "Sex does not make me uncomfortable."

"Then why look away?"

"I've got better things to do than watch people have sex."

"Like have sex yourself?"

Was he talking about sex by herself or with him? Unsure which possibility excited her more—him watching her tease herself to orgasm or being right there with her—she shook her head before either fantasy could play out in her mind.

The moaning coming from the laptop got louder, the

woman's breathless pleas rising to a feverish pitch as the man buried his face between her legs.

Cian nuzzled the back of her hair, moving to her other side. "Do these movies arouse you?"

"Not particularly." He was a doing pretty good job of that all on his own.

"You're not telling me the truth. Otherwise your scent—"

Suddenly self-conscious, she whipped around, cutting him off. "What about my scent?"

Oh boy.

Well, facing him had been a serious misstep. This close she had no choice but to angle her face up to meet his gaze, her own drawn right to his full mouth in the process. She didn't even care that a hunter's smile curved the gargoyle lips, like one who'd successfully cornered his prey and was ready to pounce. She was too busy thinking about what his mouth might taste like.

Needed to know what it tasted like.

"The movie does not—"

He reached past her, surprising her by snapping the laptop shut. "We'll get along much better if you're honest with me, sorceress. And you are aroused."

"And you are apparently suffering from some kind of post-stone stress." The pointed reminder of how he'd spent the last hundred years rolled right off his back, taking with it her last-ditch effort to get some space between them before she turned a small mistake into a colossal one.

"Very aroused," he clarified. His eyes flared, a hint of satisfaction flashing in the startling blue depths as he lowered his head.

The chain links clinked together as he gripped her hip and

pulled her close.

"Pheromones," she blurted just as his lips hovered above her own. "You're a cat. You're exciting me with your pheromones." It made perfect sense. Unfortunately the light-bulb moment was too little too late when he teased his mouth across hers.

Cian laughed softly, catching her bottom lip between his. "Hardly."

Her eyes slid shut, and then his mouth covered hers and she ceased caring about why she felt this way. The anticipation that had been snowballing inside her shattered, and she whimpered, parting her lips for him.

He cupped her nape, his fingers sinking into her skin like a molten anchor. His mouth opened wider over hers, all wet heat and hot, hungry male.

God, she couldn't get enough. Digging her fingers into his shirt, she rose up on her toes and met the decadent kiss head-on. Fire ignited in her belly the second his tongue pushed past her lips and stroked deep.

She moaned low in her throat and snaked a hand under his shirt in an instinctive urge to get closer. Cian growled and crushed her between him and the counter. The edge jammed into her back but she blocked it out.

Blocked everything out but the drugging sweep of his mouth.

Sweet pressure clenched deep in her core, intensifying when he rocked his hips, rubbing his hard length against her. She sucked at his bottom lip, then overwhelmed by just how badly she wanted him, she pushed him back half a step.

She wasn't sure which of them was more surprised that he'd given her any breathing room at all. Not that it lasted. One look at the need stamped on every inch of his handsome face and something inside her came apart.

“Cian,” she pleaded, but for what she wasn’t sure.

Thank the gods he didn’t wait for her to figure it out. Her feet left the ground as he lifted her up and set her on the counter, bringing them almost eye level. His fierce gaze promised something she couldn’t pinpoint, and then he buried his hand in her hair and claimed her mouth in another scorching kiss.

She wrapped her legs around him, moaning when his cock fit snug against her.

More. She needed so much more. Needed—

Cian pulled back, his head bowed, his hands clenched into fists at his sides. “Why?”

“What?” Her head was spinning, every cell inside her gravitating toward him even as tension thickened between them.

He raised his head. “How did you come to be in possession of Constantine’s dagger? How did you use it to curse me?”

“I...” She could barely think, let alone string together words that were supposed to make sense. Pheromones or not, the gargoyle was doing something to her. Still, she shook her head to deny the accusation.

“Don’t,” he warned, his animal nature coming through loud and clear. “Where did you find it?”

Did he think that where there was one, there’d be another? That had already occurred to her, and would have occurred to Elena as well. Her sister might be impulsive, but she would have recognized the advantage of holding on to such a coveted weapon.

Emma sighed. “I won it.” The countless treasures her sister had acquired over the years made the guess a fairly reasonable one. Gambling was the only honest way Elena made any money. She'd frequently mentioned that using magic to manipulate the cards took the fun out of gambling.

He arched a brow. She shrugged, not offering anything further.

"I meant what I said about being honest."

"Does it really matter? You're free and have the dagger in your position now."

"You and I need to come to an understanding."

"Why? Plan on locking me away in your closet indefinitely?" There was a moment of panic at the thought of being locked anywhere dark, but it was forgotten the second Cian's expression turned downright wicked.

"It doesn't have to be the closet."

"If you're under the impression that sex will make me cooperative—"

"Oh, it's not an impression."

"And I'm not some enchantress who sleeps with anything that moves." Not usually, anyway. The gargoyle was proving to be the exception, and if the telling smile that curved his lips was anything to go by, he knew it too.

"Sleeping is hardly what I had in mind."

The flash of intent in his eyes had her scooting backward until she came up against the cupboard. His grin widened, but instead of hauling her back into his arms as she'd half anticipated—half longed for—he leaned in slowly, his gaze sliding down to her mouth.

She couldn't decide what was worse—having no opportunity to stop him before he claimed her mouth completely, or seeing it coming and knowing she wanted it too much to object.

His lips brushed hers, and he groaned, the sound almost painful.

The same impulse that had driven her to stay and warm him on the roof flared anew. She cupped his cheek. "You're hurting. We should stop."

Cian shook his head, then slid his tongue along the seam of her lips before pushing inside. "Stopping hurts more. You make it all better." Another feather-light kiss. "So much better."

The worst past was that she wanted to believe him, wanted to so much that when his mouth covered hers, she told herself it might be true.

Slow to start, the kiss bounced from exploring to explosive and back. One minute they were barely breathing, pulling at each other and greedy for more, and the next he was so careful, tender—heartbreakingly so.

The contrast drove her crazy, kicking her arousal into high gear. By the time he worked her shirt up and palmed her breast, she was so on edge she bit his lip. Not hard enough to break the skin, it nevertheless got his attention.

He ran his tongue across the spot, his eyes darkening.

"I didn't mean it," she began, then stopped. She'd kept much of the truth to herself since they'd met, the least she could do was be honest about this.

Emma boldly met his gaze. "Actually, I did mean it."

He cocked a brow, but his fingers never stopped tracing the edge of her bra, dipping inside. Her eyes slammed shut, squeezing tight when he tugged her bra down and flicked his tongue across her nipple.

Sweet Avalon. Her breath hissed out, right up until he closed his lips over her, pulling her into his greedy mouth, and then her lungs stopped working altogether.

Over and over he licked the tip, only to suck her nipple back into his mouth each time. The ache deep in her sex throbbed and she brought his hand between her legs, desperate for some relief.

"Do you still deny that you're aroused?"

There was no point in denying anything when he only had to feel how damp she was. "What do you think?"

He laughed, the sound dark and seductive. "I think you want me as much as I want you."

She rolled her hips, grinding shamelessly against his palm. "You don't even like me."

"I'm keeping you here and yet you still want me."

Good point. "Okay, so we're both messed up." The last word caught in her throat the second his hand moved to her zipper.

He pulled it down and slipped a hand inside. "You're not a mess, but you *are* wet."

"A mess? I meant...forget it," she breathed, breaking off when his fingers parted her cleft.

Her nails raked the counter, seeking any kind of leverage. He found her clit instantly and swirled the pad of his thumb around the aching knot, drawing out the pleasure until every cell quivered with the need to come.

Footsteps sounded near the door. "Oh, shit."

Cian whipped around, the cat pushing close to the surface.

Why did everyone in the damn house have such bad timing? He'd been a minute, maybe a second from watching Emma come apart in his arms. Instead, he was watching his brother's mate try to back out of the room with her hand slapped over her eyes.

He'd liked Kennedy from the moment he had met her. She

and Tristan seemed like a good fit, though he doubted his brother would appreciate him taking a swipe at her to get her moving faster.

"Blame your brother," Kennedy insisted, almost reading his mind. "I told him you'd be fine." She bumped into the table, sending a stack of newspapers fluttering to the floor.

The familiar pounding in his head returned with a vengeance. "Wait." Sending Kennedy back to his brother after what she'd just walked in on would be almost as bad as making a video for everyone to see.

Which actually didn't sound so bad if it meant he could get his hands on Emma again.

Behind him, she finished adjusting her clothes and eased down next to him.

"Where is Tristan?" If his brother had come home to check on him...

"At the bar, probably a couple hundred pounds heavier by now."

At least he didn't have to worry about Tristan appearing for a while, making him grateful that mated gargoyles still needed to shift to stone to rebuild their strength or heal from any significant injuries. However, the reprieve wouldn't last long once Kennedy mentioned what he and Emma had been doing.

He scrubbed a hand down his face. "We—"

"No explanations required. Really." Kennedy dropped a pile of newspapers back on the table.

"Do you need to get back to him?"

She shrugged. "As fun as it is to watch him play statue, I'm not in a rush."

Looking at Emma made him want to send Kennedy on her way so they could pick right up where they'd left off, which was why he got the next words out before he changed his mind.

"Watch her for me?"

Kennedy frowned, her gaze sliding briefly to Emma before she nodded.

He picked up the other end of the chain he'd dropped earlier, hating the way his stomach twisted, and handed it to her. "I'll return shortly."

He couldn't bring himself to glance at Emma, though he felt her gaze following him as he crossed the room. Without another word he let himself out the patio door. Every step he took felt like he was fighting his instincts, but he forced himself away from the sorceress who clouded his thoughts until he craved only her.

Outside, Cian watched them through the window for another moment to be sure Emma wouldn't try anything. Although Kennedy had only come into her immortality and powers rather recently, he'd seen her hold her own with Tristan and Sorcha. Anyone who wasn't easily intimidated by the huntress could handle watching Emma for a little while.

He didn't plan on being gone for very long. As much as his animal half needed to run, neither man nor cat would venture too far from her. That knowledge only made him more determined to go.

He wanted his life back, damn it. He didn't want to spend any more time fixating on the sorceress.

Cian stripped out of his pants, not wanting to rip them apart as he shifted. The change came quick and familiar, his vision sharpening, muscles and bones realigning as the cat broke free.

He pawed the ground and circled the patio, then took off for the woods. There wasn't enough space to roam as far as he normally liked to. The trees didn't tower as high here as those in Avalon. Morgana's tyranny aside, he missed the world of his birth. Vaulting from tree limb to tree limb here didn't offer the same freedom as home.

For nearly an hour he moved around the perimeter of his family's property, darting from trees and back to the ground before flopping down in a sunny spot. He hadn't felt the sun on his body since Arthur's defeat and the sheer pleasure of it was all that kept him from returning to the sorceress sooner.

The only thing that would have made stretching out in the warm sun more enjoyable would have been Emma lying there next to him, running her fingers through his fur.

By the time he padded back to the patio and shifted back to dress, his stomach was rumbling. Assuming Kennedy had taken Emma back to his room, he snagged a piece of chicken from the fridge.

Whoever he was, Colonel Sanders rivaled nearly every cook he'd known in both Avalon and the human realm.

Cian left the kitchen, but instead of catching Emma's scent at the hallway leading to his room, he followed it toward the den.

"You bitch."

The huntress.

"Just wait a second," he heard Emma plead.

"You are so dead."

Snarling, Cian shoved the door open, his claws bursting through the tips of his fingers. If anyone laid one finger on her, he'd—

All three women seated on the coach turned to stare at him. No weapons were drawn. No injuries were bleeding. No huntress with a sword to Emma's throat.

He shook his head as though it would help him figure out

what the hell was going on, both with what he'd overhead and the panic that had turned his chest to a block of ice.

Kennedy whistled. "Briana is so gonna kick your ass."

Frowning, he followed her gaze to the flat box mounted on the wall next to the door. At least it had been mounted. Now it hung there, more or less, in large pieces of shredded metal.

Kennedy looked like she was fighting a grin. "Your sister just revamped the security system a month ago."

Was he supposed to know what that meant?

"You broke it," Sorcha clarified. Then she winked at him and swiveled back around to face the television, along with Kennedy.

Only Emma seemed to notice he was still in the room when the music coming from the television resumed. He could feel her tracking his progress from the corner of her eye, and enjoyed it immensely.

Just to be certain, he gave her a good, long look. "You're not hurt."

Her brows drew together. "No."

He moved around to the front of the room, first noticing the food on the table, but more importantly the absence of Sorcha's sword. Even though she was no longer hunting rogue immortals, she was seldom unarmed, according to Briana.

"You didn't attack her."

Sorcha shook her head. "Just threw her off a cliff."

He tried to take comfort in the fact that women were just as confusing now as a hundred years ago. "What?"

"The game," Emma said gently, motioning to the screen behind him.

"Your new pet pushed my Mario into the man-eating plant." Sorcha spared him a brief look before tapping buttons on the piece of plastic she held in her hands.

"Only after your Luigi shoved her into the lava." Kennedy snagged a pretzel from the bowl and popped it into her mouth.

"A game," he repeated, the cat inside him finally starting to calm. There hadn't been a threat to Emma.

Instead the three of them were playing a video game. Together. He'd only been gone an hour and already they were befriending her? The sorceress who'd left him in stone for a century?

"She's not my pet," he snapped.

"Really?" Sorcha nudged the end of the gold and silver links with her foot. "Because that looks like a chain to me." She glanced at Kennedy, who nodded.

"You were the one who put the chain on her to begin with."

The huntress shrugged as though that detail was irrelevant at this point. "You should at least get her a studded collar to match if you're planning on keeping her awhile."

Kennedy coughed and looked at the screen.

He stared Sorcha down, half hoping to provoke the huntress. He'd only feel marginally guilty for tangling with his brother's mate if it managed to loosen the tension that had tightened to a stranglehold the moment he'd thought Emma was in trouble. And if Cale wanted to kick his ass for it later, so much the better. Right about now he had as much energy as three gargoyles and needed a way to burn it off before it burned him up.

But Sorcha didn't take the bait, arching a brow and smiling like she knew something he didn't.

Whose side was she on, anyway?

"Let's go," he growled at Emma.

"We're on our way out too," Sorcha added, her grin

widening. "Don't forget your leash though."

He snapped the other end of the chain up but Emma was already ahead of him. Impatient to get out of there, he didn't bother to say goodbye.

"You're welcome," Kennedy called out as the pair joined them in the hall, but thankfully headed in the opposite direction. "Later, Emma."

The two laughed and he swore he heard them say something about wondering how long he'd have his head stuffed up his ass.

He hadn't calmed down much by the time he reached his rooms. He needed to go for a run, or hit something. Anything to defuse the rising upheaval that left him on edge.

Emma said nothing, her face no longer as relaxed as it had been in the den.

Damn it, he would not feel guilty over that. She'd stolen a hundred years of his life and hadn't shown even an ounce of remorse. Making it all the worse was how easily she'd charmed everyone. First him, then his brothers' mates—and they'd helped track her down.

If it took him being an ass to make Emma grateful he hadn't locked her in the cellar for the next millennia, that was fine with him. The angrier he was, the less he wanted to strip her down and trace every inch of her with his tongue—

Emma swiveled around without warning, and he nearly ran over her. She huffed out a breath, but quickly got her bearings—too quickly—and backed up.

Instantly, he recognized the determined glimmer in her eyes, the same he'd glimpsed earlier in the kitchen.

"Was there something you wanted to say?" Or do? Or touch?

She squared her shoulders. “Make up your mind.”

“Excuse me?”

“You need to decide what you plan to do to me.”

“To you?” Angry, aroused or just plain out of his mind, the list was truly endless.

She didn’t back down, not even when he deliberately tried to crowd her, propping one hand on the wall and leaning in until her back came up against it.

“However you plan on getting even, you need to make up your mind.”

“That sounds like an awfully big threat from a rather powerless sorceress.”

She flinched, then her cheeks deepened to a dark pink, as did the tip of her nose. She jerked her hand up. “I won’t always be wearing this, gargoyle.”

“So I should be nice to you, is that it?”

Her chin came up another notch, but she said nothing.

“How nice are you looking for exactly?” He planted his other hand on the opposite side of her. “Nice like I was in the kitchen or very, very nice?”

She slammed her palm into his chest.

He grinned at the aggressive play even as the most primitive parts of him hungered to dominate her in every way. Her scent was driving him crazy. It was all he could do not to tuck his face against her throat and inhale her. The longer they stood so close, the harder he found it to remember anything but the taste of her.

“Whatever it is, just—” her breath hissed out when he couldn’t help himself and ran his thumb from the base of her throat up to her chin, “—get on with it already.” The last few words were only a whisper.

He watched her mouth. "Is there some other place you need to be?" Fascinated with the flutter of her pulse, he opened his mouth over her warm skin.

She closed her eyes and the fingers she planted against his chest curled into his shirt. "It won't be long before I'm tracked here. Do you think I have no one who cares enough to look for me?"

The cat snarled possessively, but the man only nipped at her. "An army could come and it wouldn't matter." He waited until she looked at him to be sure she understood perfectly. "I have no intention of letting you go."

Chapter Four

"You would risk your family to keep me?"

For all the practice she had at masking her fear—thanks to Elena—the gargoyle's steel-edged conviction made it hard not to take him seriously. As worried as she'd been over her fate, some small part of her had dared to hope he might willingly release her.

The look on his face, the unwavering blue depths locked on her, told her he meant every word. He really had no intention of releasing her.

"My family can handle themselves."

She swallowed past the momentary panic clawing at her throat. "So revenge is all that matters to you?" She certainly hadn't gotten that vibe when she'd touched his belongings and experienced those memories.

"Not all that matters, no." He dragged his shirt over his head and tossed it behind him.

"Whoa there, Chippendale. Let's keep this PG rated."

Unfazed, he moved his hand to the fly of his jeans, drawing her attention down his toned abs—and how had she missed those on the roof?

"Is there a problem?"

Hell yeah, there was a problem. She just couldn't

remember exactly what it was as the button gaped open just a fraction.

Focusing, she went with the obvious. "You just took your shirt off."

"And yours is next."

"In your dreams, gargoyle." She slipped around him, finding it easier to keep a clear head when she wasn't pinned between him and the wall.

He tugged his zipper down and circled her, pausing behind her long enough to whisper, "In my dreams the only thing covering your body is me."

Her stomach grew hot at the image that unfolded in her mind. She shook her head to erase it as much to discourage him—as if that were possible—and preferably before the jeans riding low on his hips slid any lower.

Avalon help her, there was no way he was wearing any underwear beneath them.

She needed to stay focused on finding a way out of this mess, preferably with her clothing intact.

Given the way the corners of his mouth tipped up, as if amused by her white-knuckled grip on her shirt, the odds didn't seem to be in her favor. That fact alone spurred her retreat.

Cian tensed like an animal about to take down its prey, but after a few feet, he still hadn't moved. How was it that he managed to make her feel like she was being stalked when he hadn't taken a single step in her direction?

She searched his face, finally understanding the wicked glimmer in his eyes. He was enjoying it. He wanted her to run, wanted to catch her.

Which only forced her to acknowledge that she wanted to be caught.

Caught. Kissed. Touched.

And it was all so damn crazy. She didn't do one-night stands with men under normal circumstances, let alone with one who was casually eyeing the chain she dragged along the floor like it was part of the trap he couldn't wait to spring.

"I am not some sex slave."

When he took a step toward her, she wished she hadn't said a damn thing.

"You're right about that," he drawled innocently, and she scrambled back another step, realizing too late he was herding her toward his bedroom.

"Slaves," he continued, "need to be coerced in the beginning. You want it. Want me."

A hint of uncertainty echoed beneath all that slick feline arrogance, surprising her. Distracting her. Otherwise she might have noticed how quickly he closed the distance between them, forcing her to tip her head back to meet his gaze. He towered over her five-foot-four frame, but she didn't find it as intimidating as she should have given the magic-nulling handcuff locked around her wrist.

Everything about the situation left her at a disadvantage, but she refused to play the submissive female.

He stared at her throat before finally lifting his hand and tracing the soft hollow, then moving on to her collarbone. The teasing brush of his thumb was at odds with the tension she felt radiating from him.

"You didn't deny that you want me." His hands slid beneath her jacket and over her shoulders.

"And give you a reason to prove I was lying?"

He laughed, and the rough sound washed over her. A little dazed by his smile, she was slow to process her jacket sliding down to her arms.

Her eyes snapped open—when the hell had she closed them?—and she stumbled back. He might have been too distracted when she'd been in the shower to realize how few tracings she had, but risking it a second time was a really bad idea. It wouldn't take him long to realize the cuff would null any ability to mask her tracings.

A tug on her wrist pulled her forward. She immediately retreated, stepping inside the dark bedroom at her back.

Could he see well enough to notice her tracings—or lack thereof—in the dark?

He stopped in the doorway, the light behind him casting his face in shadows. Maybe she'd been a little premature with the whole not-intimidated thing. She managed another step, and he countered with another tug on the chain until she was forced to meet him halfway.

"Cian."

He stopped, only a foot away now. "Again." He stepped forward, and her thighs connected with his.

"I don't—"

"My name. Say it again."

Her lips parted soundlessly.

"Please."

Inches separated them. "Cian."

His palm caressed her jaw, guiding her closer. "Again," he murmured.

"Ci—"

He slanted his mouth across hers. Soft and hot, the lazy kiss stoked a low fire in her belly. It was impossible not to part her lips and welcome him deeper, sinking into him.

He groaned, nipping at her bottom lip and getting closer.

And then everything shot sideways. She thought it was just in her head until Cian's arm snapped around her and they went down hard. He took the brunt of the impact when they hit the floor.

Hearing the chain clink somewhere behind her, Emma realized it had tripped them. Catching her breath, she stared down at him, increasingly aware of the way she was sprawled across his chest. Without her jacket providing any kind of buffer, there was no way to deny how good it felt to be tucked against him.

Carefully, he brushed her hair to the side, his fingers sliding through the dark strands.

"Do you have any idea how beautiful you are?"

She shook her head. She'd never considered herself more than average, especially when standing next to her twin. Elena's natural glow drew men like lambs to the heart-breaking slaughter.

But the way Cian was looking at her...like something from a dream whose details had faded and left only the feeling that she wanted to relive it over and over again.

"After a hundred years, I'm betting you'd find even a blow-up doll beautiful."

Cian's mouth fell open. "A child's toy is meant to explode in this century?"

"No. That's not...I mean..." She closed her eyes at the feel of his fingers rubbing along her neck. "That's really distracting, you know."

He rolled to trap her beneath him, then ran his mouth along the same path. "How about this?"

"I can still string a sentence together." Barely. Another

minute of this and he'd have to peel her off the floor. God, the only thing worse than the gargoyle holding her against her will was how much she was enjoying it.

Avalon help her, she really was worse than an enchantress. "You and I... We need to stop... We can't do this."

He opened his mouth over the hollow at the base of her throat. "Can. Most definitely are."

"So you'd force me?"

"Did I force you to put your arms around my neck, sorceress?"

Her gaze darted to the traitorous hands linked behind his neck. A low growl stopped her from releasing her hold on him entirely.

"And afterward you'll dispose of me, or maybe keep me chained up here until the next time?" Maybe if she clung to the latter possibility, she would stop aching to feel his mouth on hers again.

"Then we'll do it again." He pulled her skin between his lips, sucking softly. "And again."

Pure carnal heat streamed through her and she arched beneath him. A sexy groan of approval rumbled in his chest. Catching her mouth with his, Cian kissed her long and deep, coaxing a desperate moan from her lips. And desperate was the only way to describe the need crackling under her skin.

"Admit how much you want me, Emma."

"I think your ego is already big enough, gargoyle." She planted a hand against his chest, not expecting—or really wanting—him to budge when she gave him a half-hearted push.

He surprised her by rolling to his back again and dragging her with him. He caught her hips, pulling her until she brushed the hard length of him.

They both moaned, and she straddled him, instinctively rocking back until the head of his cock pressed against her.

His fingers dug into her, holding her still. His expression darkened, with pleasure or pain she wasn't sure. Then he caught the ends of her shirt and jerked it over her head. And Avalon help her, she didn't even try to stop him.

So beautiful.

Cian let his head drop back to the floor, a little bit dazed by the female hovering over him. Her cheeks were flushed, her lips damp from his mouth, her eyes...for a moment he thought he saw flecks of purple glint in the dim lighting.

He ran his gaze over her shoulders, to the black lace molded to her breasts. Sliding a finger beneath the strap, he tugged her down until his mouth met the sexy curve of her neck.

The cat growled at her tantalizing scent, wanting to leave its mark on her. That alone should have sent him scrambling from beneath her. He'd never been in a hurry to find his mate, focused first on helping Arthur build a strong, peaceful vision of Avalon, and then on finding the daggers that would return their king to them.

But if finding his mate felt half as incredible as he did right now—like he might go out of his mind if he didn't get another taste of her lips or glimpse her stunning smile—he'd been wrong to prefer his life as it was.

Holding her gaze, Cian tugged the material down until he glimpsed the dark pink tip.

Emma went still, her eyes sliding shut. His own drifted closed as his jaw grazed the curve of her breast and he flicked his tongue across her nipple.

Her breath hitched, and he opened his mouth over the tip, pulling her deep between his lips.

Digging her nails into his shoulders, she cried out, and the sound unleashed a rush of molten lust inside him. He groaned, pulling her closer and knowing it wouldn't be enough.

Not until she was his.

He cupped her nape, dragging her down to meet his mouth. The sheer rightness that uncoiled inside him as her lips parted for his made him burn even hotter. He'd always assumed being burned alive would be a painful way to go, but the feeling of Emma tunneling her fingers into his hair and moaning against his mouth was more than worth the heat sizzling through his veins.

The kiss moved from drugging to wild, and some place in between as he unsnapped her trousers and pushed them down over her hips.

Her thigh brushed his arousal, and his jaw clenched.

"What's wrong? Did I hurt you?"

Only in the best way possible. He shook his head, the effort it took to speak coherently with the cat riding him so hard was better spent getting her naked.

"Cian?" When she wiggled on top of him again—trying to get up?—he groaned, and she caught on. And did it again. One deliberate, sexy arch of her spine that made all the right places rub against him.

She nipped his jaw, and he growled. He doubted she even knew what she was doing to him every time she dragged her teeth across his skin. The temptress didn't leave his mouth until he finally stripped her clothing off, along with the scrap of material fitted to her ass, and pulled her up his body.

Her nipple whispered across his cheek, and he paused long

enough to draw her into his mouth, sucking soft and slow.

"Please," she murmured.

He didn't ask what she wanted, hoping it was the same thing he did. She caught his arm, uncertain, as he tugged her along. Only when her knees straddled his shoulders did he ease his hold on her.

"Wait."

He didn't. He curved his hands around her parted thighs and lifted his head for his first full taste of her. Her damp folds parted beneath his tongue, and she cried out. That right there was what he wanted, hungered for. To touch her and feel her tremble all over.

Licking deeper, he inched his mouth higher, laving the slick knot at her center.

"Yes." She flexed to rub against his lips, her breath hissing out the moment he pulled her into his mouth.

"Cian, don't...don't stop."

Not even if she begged him to. Not until he made it so incredible for her that she'd fall apart. Maybe then he'd be able to slow down for a moment, instead of want to devour every inch of her. No female had ever gotten so deep under his skin, and acknowledging that only made him that much more determined to find out why this one captivated him like no other.

Opening his mouth a little more, he kissed and teased her, slowing only when her thighs squeezed him.

She edged away from him, her moan almost a sob.

Satisfaction curled through him, making him even harder. He wasn't sure how that was even possible considering the heightened state of arousal he'd been stuck in for the last three days.

With the most decadent revenge in mind, he eased away, kissing her inner thigh and slowly working his way back. So slow every whisper of satiny skin across his lips sent a hot burst of need straight to his cock.

By the gods, he was in trouble. And he wasn't even inside her yet. Laying a hot, wet path through her folds, he circled the sweet center of her, laving until she cried out.

After rocking gently against his mouth as her climax faded, she slid down, tucking her face against his throat. He used the time to try and get a hold of himself—and gave up before she'd even caught her breath.

Not even the sound of her chain dragging across the floor as he hauled her to her feet could stop him from finishing what they'd starting in the kitchen. She fit too perfectly against his body, his mouth, his heart—

Everything inside him skidded to a stop. Right up until Emma looped her arms around his neck and sucked his bottom lip between hers. The teasing nip and slide of her mouth across his threw a switch in his head, wiping out the insane thought he hadn't been able to finish.

Later maybe, when the stunning female with haunting gray eyes wasn't pressed against him and kissing her way down his chest.

Sweet Avalon.

Unable to make it the rest of the way across the room, to the bed, he took the few steps needed and backed her against the wall. The predator in him growled in triumph at cornering her, trapping her.

Emma's chest rose and fell in quick bursts. "This isn't... I didn't expect it to be like this."

Neither did he.

Slanting his mouth across hers, he tugged his trousers down, and the second his shaft brushed smooth, hot skin, he groaned. She didn't wait for him to nudge her legs apart, reaching out instead and closing her hand around his cock.

Fuck.

For a second he felt like he had on the roof. Disoriented and overwhelmed, and much too close to losing his mind. And then she pumped her hand up the length of him, and pleasure rushed in.

"Closer," she whispered against his mouth.

With her hand guiding him to her sex, they were about to get as close as two people could. He cupped her ass, massaging his way to her hip and then down to lift her leg. She hooked it around him, sighing a little as he fit against her.

In one smooth thrust he was inside her, sinking all the way to heaven. Her nails dug into his biceps, and when she released the breath she'd been holding—and she wasn't the only one—her body relaxed, letting him get a little deeper.

He dropped his forehead to hers, trying to remember how to make his lungs work, then he withdrew and pumped his hips to fill her again and again.

Instinct rushed in with his animal half's need to dominate, and for a long minute he fought it. Fought it until his muscles ached from holding back. One last slow push inside her to savor the clench of her slick sex around him, the incredible sounds she made against his mouth, and then he thrust harder.

Her mouth found the curve of his neck, where she pressed hot, wild kisses in between each soft cry of pleasure. Both of which were testing his ability not to explode inside her any second. And he wasn't ready for it to end. Not yet. Maybe not ever.

"It feels like I've been waiting forever to find you." It had to be one of the most insane thoughts he'd ever shared with a female. Even more insane was feeling it right down to his bones.

He searched her eyes, unsure what response he was looking for—hoping for?—until a slow smile lit up her face. Crushing his mouth over hers, he lifted her a little higher, getting as deep inside her as he could.

At some point both of Emma's legs were wrapped around him, their hands linked before she needed to hold onto him as he pounded into her. Next to them the painting rattled, falling on the floor a few seconds later.

"There," she hissed. "Right..." She moaned into his mouth, the hot walls of her sex rippling around him as she came a moment later.

"Emma," he growled, pumping his hips faster...faster.

He dropped his head to the crook of her shoulder, burying himself inside her and holding on as his release slammed into him.

"Cian?" Her voice soothed him, and he slowly raised his head, wondering how long he'd been lost in thought as his body came back down.

"I wasn't expecting that," she admitted quietly, lifting her gaze to meet his. "Wasn't expecting you."

Serious gray eyes tunneled straight into his soul, flipping a panic button in his head.

Even as he eased away from her, need clawed through him. The cat wanted to curl around her, stay with its mate—

He stumbled back.

No. It wasn't possible. She couldn't be his mate. She may have been all he'd thought about for the last three days, but if she were truly his mate he would have felt that instant awareness of her the night she'd cursed him.

"What did you do to me?"

"What are you talking about?"

He caught her arms.

"You're hurting me."

"Tell me what you did to me. What kind of spell did you cast?"

Confused, she shook her head. "I didn't cast any spell."

"Undo it. Now."

"Evidently you and your brother have been drinking the same Kool-Aid." She flattened her palm over his chest. "Do you really think that what you felt, what we both felt, was because of some spell?" Her tone dared him to disagree.

So he did. "You turned me to stone. If I felt a fraction of the hunger for another female that I feel for you, do you think I would be here?"

She flinched and shoved him back a step, seeming surprised when he retreated. "I did not enchant you."

"You're lying." There was no other explanation.

She jerked on the chain cuffed to one wrist. "Maybe you didn't get the memo, but this makes it impossible to cast."

"So you found a way around it."

"Clearly spending a century as a rock left you a few pebbles short."

It took him a minute to get her meaning. The sorceress talked circles around him. To purposely confuse him more than he already was?

She shoved past him.

He growled and reached for her, stopping when he realized how badly he wanted to be closer to her. "Where are you going?"

"To the bathroom," she snapped. She slammed the door behind her.

Cursing, he rubbed his hands over his face. Whatever Emma had done left him turned inside out, and she had done something, hadn't she? She was powerful enough to channel the dagger's magic, had used it to curse him. Any sorceress capable of that might have been able to find a way around the magic-nulling cuff she wore.

The cat raked the edges of his mind, feeling betrayed by Cian's thoughts. Torn in two, he prowled the length of the room. Maybe she hadn't found a way around the cuff. Maybe this was all part of the original spell, a safeguard to prevent him from hurting her in case the curse was broken.

He swung around to face the bathroom. "Emma?"

She didn't answer him.

He deliberately softened his tone. "Emma?" He knew yelling at her was not the best way to get answers. At least that's what he told himself when he knocked on the door.

No response.

"Damn it, Emma. Talk to me."

When she continued to ignore him, he walked in. A blur of white sliced across his peripheral vision, and then pain exploded across his skull and everything went dark.

Chapter Five

"Are you out of your mind?"

"A few pebbles short apparently." Cian tried once more to pass his sister, and each time Briana blocked his path.

"It's only been two weeks, Cian. It's not long enough. You're not ready to go gallivanting after a sorceress."

"If I don't find her, I'm going to go out of my mind." And that was putting it mildly.

He didn't say any more than that. Didn't want Briana worrying about him any more than she already was. If she knew he was hardly sleeping, afraid to dream about Emma, or knew how much time he spent on the roof, lost in his few memories of her, she'd be afraid of more than whether or not he could handle a world still so foreign to him.

Briana threw a helpless glance over Cian's shoulder. "Do something."

Behind him, his brother Cale arched a brow. "Like what exactly? Ground him?"

"He's not ready."

"According to you," Cian pointed out, though he wasn't certain she was entirely wrong. But facing the fast-moving world outside his family's home had to be better than hungering for a female that wasn't truly his.

They'd all hoped the spell would fade after Emma had pulled her vanishing act. Though he still hadn't been able to live down the concussion she'd given him using the ceramic toilet tank cover.

Weeks later and he longed for her just as much as he had those first few moments when he'd awoken and realized her fading scent was too buried beneath a hundred neighborhood smells to track her.

Sorcha hadn't had a whole lot of success either, and the oracle, a rare clairvoyant immortal, who'd told Cale how to find Emma in the first place, didn't have much to offer. But Cian couldn't sit and wait for someone else to find her. She was his problem, and if it took staking out every place she'd regularly frequented in the last fifty years to find her, he would do it as long as it took.

The alternative, pining away for a mate he couldn't call his own, wasn't an option. Not when gargoyles embraced their animal halves entirely, becoming the Forgotten for a lot less than a spell.

After Camelot had fallen to Morgana's army, Cian had watched the grief that consumed a few of his fellow soldiers lead them to surrender their humanity to their beast halves. Once those ties were severed, they struggled to recognize friend from foe, and if they didn't strike out on their own soon after it happened, someone often ended up dead.

"You can't go alone," Briana argued.

"Tristan has Pendragon's to run and Cale and Sorcha have other daggers to find."

"Then I'll go."

"No, you won't." He'd deliberately waited until close to sunrise to leave, anticipating her stubbornness. "The sun will be up in less than an hour. And you were the one who warned me about stone gargoyles stuck in the middle of an intersection."

Briana poked him in the chest. "Don't you dare use that tone with me."

"What tone?"

"The same one you used when you ran off and joined the Guard when we were barely more than cubs."

"For the thousandth time, you couldn't have come. Females weren't allowed."

"Thank the gods this realm isn't as chauvinistic as ours."

Cian snorted, but before he could reply, Cale stepped between them. "Is this where I have to step in and threaten to toss both of you around by the scruff of your necks?"

"I'd pay a small fortune to see that." Sorcha strolled into the room. "Or more specifically the part where they team up to take you down."

Cale scoffed, hauling his mate into his arms. "I can take you down."

Sorcha nodded. "When I let you."

Cale growled softly at the challenge, and both Cian and Briana rolled their eyes.

Turning her back on the couple, Briana caught his arm. "You don't need to do this alone. I can—" She broke off, glancing at Cale.

"You can what?"

Her brows drew together. "Help," she finally answered, leaving Cian with the impression she'd wanted to say something else.

"I need to do this on my own. She may not be my mate, but the cat thinks she is. Someday you'll get it."

Pain blinked across her face so briefly he might have imagined it.

"Hey," he began, unsure of what he should apologize for. He'd swear he spent half his adolescence telling Briana he was sorry for something, whenever he wasn't dragging her into whatever trouble he'd found.

A smile curved her lips but didn't quite reach her eyes. "Just be careful and if you need me, call. Promise me."

He pulled her into his arms for a fierce hug, the sudden tightness in his throat preventing him from responding right away.

Briana's eyes were suspiciously shiny when she drew back. "And if you're stupid enough to let that sorceress curse you again, just know that I'll be using your stone ass to hang my lingerie on."

"Nice," Sorcha quipped.

Cale shook his head at her. "Don't even think about it."

The huntress grinned at him. "C'mon. I'd bet you'd look fabulous in a little black or red lace."

Shooting his sister a dark look, Cale turned Sorcha back the way she'd come. "Thank you for that."

Briana smiled. "Anytime. Don't worry, I won't mention how good of a target you'd make the next time she and Nessa are playing paintball."

Cian cringed on his brother's behalf. Having had the—pleasure? Misfortune?—of meeting Sorcha's huntress friend, he sympathized with Cale.

Sorcha held her hand to her ear in what Cian had learned was some universal sign for *call me.*

Yeah, his brother had his hands full with that one.

"Briana's right about watching your ass." Cale clapped him

on the back.

Cian grinned. "I'll miss you too."

Briana shoved her hands in her pockets when Cale and Sorcha left the room. "I mean it, call me. I'm number one on your speed dial."

"I know."

She nodded, ducking in for another quick hug. "Give her hell, Cian."

He planned on giving Emma a lot more than that, even if it killed him.

Emma stared at the cards on the blackjack table in front of her as the dealer waited for her. She glanced at the cards face up in front of the other players, quickly adding the values in her head and ending with a positive count. With a higher number of face cards still in the deck, she had the mathematical advantage. Doubling her bet, she then tapped for another card.

The dealer laid a Jack of Spades, bringing her total to twenty and beating the house.

"You're moping, you know."

Emma tinkered with the stack of chips she'd just won, looking anywhere in the busy casino but at her aunt. Surrogate aunt anyway, according to the woman who so closely shared her hair and eye color that they were often confused as mother and daughter.

Twenty years ago, when Elena had been at the height of her rebellion, they'd found themselves stranded on the side of the road in the middle of nowhere. Leah had stopped to offer them a ride, and although Emma had half-expected her twin to charm the woman out of her vehicle and whatever cash she had, they ended up hitting it off. Probably had something to do with both Leah and Elena being free spirits.

When Leah had offered them a place to stay, they'd quickly agreed, wanting to stay off their father's radar for a while. Since then, they'd both made a habit of dropping in on Leah whenever they were in Vegas. Which was a lot.

Leah had eventually recognized them as something more than human—Emma was convinced there was Fae blood in her family line somewhere—but not until a pissed-off sorcerer cornered them did they tell her the truth. In true Leah fashion, the revelation rolled right off her back and they carried on with their evening as though nothing had changed.

"It's a man, isn't it?" Leah stood and scooped up her chips.

Emma kept her attention on the table, setting her initial bet and waiting for the dealer to come back to her.

What in the hell had she been thinking when Leah asked her to tag along this afternoon? She would have been better off staying at Leah's, curled up with a stack of DVDs and enough fudge to pave the Las Vegas Strip.

But no, she hadn't wanted Leah to think she was moping—which had turned out *beautifully*—so she'd come along. She'd assumed Leah would vanish within the first twenty minutes, right around the time she inevitably spotted a potential candidate for her next husband.

As far as Emma knew, they were only ever candidates. As much as Leah adored men in general, she had never really gotten over her first husband.

"You'll tell me eventually, you know." Leah sent another flirtatious smile to the man two seats down from Emma. "Does Elena know you had your heart broken?"

"I did not have my heart broken," she hissed, sending the dealer an apologetic look for Leah's constant distractions.

He stared back at her. She frowned, then realized he was waiting for her. Doing the math, she doubled down and motioned to stand when he laid down an eight of hearts.

"Trampled a bit, then." Leah shrugged as though it was all the same.

"Hardly." She might have been foolish enough to give in to the gargoyle but there was a world of difference between love and lust. Hardcore, hot-all-the-way-to-her-toes lust. The kind she hadn't been able to stop thinking about—whenever she wasn't looking over her shoulder for him, or imagining him dangling over the catacomb fire pits.

"Good," Leah murmured. "Get right back up on the horse, I say."

Since she'd been on a roll for a while and caught the dealer glancing in the direction of the pit boss a couple of times, she pulled her next bet back and intentionally busted. Counting cards wasn't illegal, but casinos were well known for banning suspected card counters from the premises.

"And if there was ever a stallion in need of mounting, it's him."

Emma choked on her drink, afraid to look at whatever male specimen had caught Leah's attention. Instead, she checked the time on her cell phone, ignoring the lingering redness on her wrist from the cuff it had taken her a week to get off, and only with a Fae's help. She now owed Dolan and didn't look forward to him collecting any time soon.

"Oh," Leah added a moment later, sounding disappointed.

"What, spot a wedding ring?"

Setting up for the next hand, the dealer cracked a smile.

"No, but I'd say he's off the market."

Assuming the guy in question had just been joined by his

wife or girlfriend, Emma debated whether or not to give up her seat after the next hand.

"Room for one more?" a familiar voice said to her right.

Emma froze, afraid to look. Awareness licked up her spine, and she slowly lifted her head. Her gaze collided with Cian's.

"Giddy up," Leah quipped.

"Where are you going?" Without taking her eyes off Cian, she reached her hand back to catch Leah, but she'd already backed up.

"The craps tables are calling my name."

Hundred bucks said she only went as far as the bar, where she could keep an eye on Emma and her stallion.

Emma watched, not a little dumbstruck, as Cian joined the game. The entire scene felt like something out of a nightmare. If it had been a fantasy, he would have been naked, or at the very least without a shirt.

He gave her a knowing smirk, as if he could tell she'd just been thinking about his chest.

How in the hell had he found her? She'd been careful not to stay in any one place for more than a day or two, or tell anyone where she was going next, and neither she or Elena ever told anyone about Leah.

He cocked his head, lifting a hand to probe the place she'd nailed him. "Still attached."

"Unfortunately," she murmured, forcing her attention back to her cards.

And to think she'd been worried she'd struck him too hard that night in his bathroom. She might have been crazy enough to think she'd felt some kind of connection to him, but his anger following the best sex of her life had helped her come to her senses. She'd never blindsided anyone the way she had

Cian when she'd lain in wait for him with the heavy toilet tank cover, and the guilt afterward had nearly paralyzed her.

Remembering the fury in his eyes, though, had gotten her ass moving in the end. Too bad it hadn't been enough to erase the memory of being with him altogether.

It feels like I've been waiting forever to find you.

She'd believed him. As crazy and naïve as it was, in the moment, she had felt the same, and the only person she was furious with—other than herself—over the whole mess was Elena. And when she caught up with her twin...

"Ma'am?"

She scanned the last cards played from beneath lowered lashes and motioned for another card of her own, then stayed at nineteen. She counted the seconds until the hand ended and she could get away from the table.

Cian motioned for another card. "Hit me." He leaned forward, his attention on Emma. "Oh wait, you already did that."

She smiled sweetly. "And enjoyed every second."

He scowled, and she basked in the minor victory as his total hit twenty-two and she beat both him and the house.

Gathering up her chips, she slid away from the table, knowing the thirty-second head start Cian gave her meant nothing. He hadn't tracked her to this point to let her walk away.

The gargoyle proved her instincts were dead on when he tipped the dealer and trailed after her. She headed toward the slot machines, glancing over her shoulder to find his purposeful strides bordered on stalking. He weaved around tables and people the way an animal leaped over obstacles in the woods.

They both knew it was just a matter of time before he made

his move. That didn't stop her from zigzagging between rows of blinking slot machines. So intent on getting some distance between them, she stopped paying attention to her surroundings and lost track of where she was in the casino.

Chancing a quick glance behind her, she slowly came to a stop. He wasn't behind her, so she waited a beat, anticipating him rounding the corner any second.

He didn't.

Could she have actually lost him? She started to dismiss the possibility before remembering he'd probably never stepped foot in a casino before today. He could have learned the rules of modern blackjack from watching television or online, which meant the casino's design and intentional lack of easy-to-recognize landmarks could have disorientated him.

Hope flared in her chest, and she whirled around intent on grabbing Leah and getting the hell out of there. She dug in her bag for her cell phone, keeping an eye out for Cian.

Ducking into a small alcove between two rows of slots, her fingers fumbled over the keys while texting Leah to meet her outside. She slipped her phone back in her bag and froze as she caught a glimpse of Cian searching for her. She held her breath, letting it out slowly when he moved on without spotting her.

Heading in the opposite direction, Emma collided with a twenty-something woman on crutches.

Crap. "Sorry about that."

"No problem." The woman smiled, and Emma paused, momentarily distracted by her smile.

With long, wavy black hair, a flawless complexion and a full pouty mouth, the woman was gorgeous, plain and simple. Probably a model or a showgirl. "I should have been paying more attention." Not an easy feat with a vengeful gargoyle hot on her trail.

"I just broke my foot a week ago and still feel a little like Godzilla lumbering around whenever I get in tight spaces." She held out her hand for the crutch Emma had knocked into a planter.

Careful not to shove it at the woman, she forced a smile. "You might want to steer clear of the buffet then. The starving masses don't think twice about crowding people when food is involved."

She laughed, started past Emma, then stopped. "I don't suppose you might know where the bathroom is, would you?"

"No, sorry." She glanced around for Cian.

"I'm the one who's sorry. You look like you're in a hurry and here I am babbling. I have a bad habit of doing that when I'm nervous. This is my first trip to Las Vegas and my boyfriend has disappeared, and I had one too many cocktails, hence my search for the bathroom...and I'm doing it again, aren't I? Sorry."

"Don't worry about it."

"Okay." She smiled again, but it didn't light up her face like before, and Emma swore she looked a little worried.

There wasn't time to play Good Samaritan, and yet the way the other woman worried her necklace, the same way Leah did whenever she was pretending she wasn't overwhelmed by something, made Emma cave. "You know, I've been looking for the bathroom myself. Maybe between the two of us, we can find it." Sooner rather than later, preferably.

The other woman's smile brightened. "Great. Two sets of eyes are better than one, right?" She fell into step with Emma, not complaining that Emma was probably walking too quickly for someone still getting used to crutches.

Feeling a little guilty over that, she tried to slow down just a bit.

The woman glanced behind them, following Emma's gaze. "Is something wrong?"

"Nothing an overdose of catnip won't fix."

"I'd help you out but I traded my last bag for a mimosa earlier."

Emma grinned, a little relieved when she spotted a sign for the washrooms. Leaving the cover of the slot machines instantly made her feel vulnerable, and she wanted to get to Leah now.

"Good luck finding your boyfriend."

"Thanks, I think I'll need it." She motioned at the floor with one of her crutches. "There's a token by your foot. Could be lucky."

Emma bent and picked it up without thinking, belatedly bracing herself for the memories that would come with it.

Nothing.

"It's never been played before," she mused aloud.

The woman cocked her head. "How do you know that?"

"Just a feeling." She shoved the token in her pocket, nodding as the other woman smiled and disappeared into the washrooms.

Eager to get moving, Emma turned around—and ran smack into Cian.

His hand curled around her elbow, and her skin grew hot beneath his touch. "Emma."

The sound of her name on his lips, heavy with longing, tugged at her. She didn't fight him when he drew her closer. Her forehead brushed his cheek, rough with a day's growth of stubble, as his palm settled at the small of her back.

His lips grazed her ear. "You shouldn't have run."

"You shouldn't have come after me."

His hand trailed up her spine, his fingers brushing her nape, making it so much harder to sound indifferent. Apparently the pep talks she'd given herself about her conflicting emotions for Cian hadn't been half as effective as she'd thought. Not with him standing so close and smelling so good and making it impossible to forget that she knew what his naked body felt like pressed up against hers.

Growling low and sexy, he dropped his head until his lips skimmed her cheek. "If you get any more aroused, I will take you right here without a second thought. I need to be inside you that much."

As far as threats went, it was damn effective. Her panties grew damp instantly.

"Fuck," he breathed, his mouth hot on her skin.

Her eyes slid shut and she ceased to think about anything but how incredible his lips felt burning a path straight to her mouth.

Behind them someone squealed and the sound of a slot machine emptying broke them apart.

His gaze darkened. "You and I need to talk."

"Well, since you said please," she drawled.

He sidestepped when she made a move to go around him. "Now."

"Do you know what's missing here, gargoyle?"

He cocked his head, his eyes much too intense for the lazy once-over he gave her. "You're not wearing any undergarments?"

She might have smiled if he didn't sound both hopeful and annoyed. Mostly annoyed.

Deciding to use their proximity to make her point, she looped one arm around his neck. His spine straightened, right up until she ran her fingers through the ends of his hair, and his eyes slid shut.

"Feel that," she murmured, forcing herself to ignore how good he felt so she wouldn't lose her only advantage. "That happens to be my bare wrist on your skin, the one no longer hindered by your little handcuff."

His eyes snapped open, and she dropped her arm.

"I see that we're on the same page now, so how about you stop ordering me around?"

"You would reveal yourself to the humans here?"

Not a chance, but she'd always been good when it came to bluffing. It was one of the few things she was better at than Elena. "What makes you think I can't make them forget anything they shouldn't see?"

He wasn't buying it. She could read it plain as day on his face, and yet he didn't call her on it. Instead his brows drew together, like he was puzzling something out that didn't add up.

"You intrigue me, sorceress."

"And is that why you're here? Because I intrigue you? Because I was under the impression it probably had something to do with the colossal goose egg I must have given you. Among other things."

She waited for him to scowl or say something to piss her off. He wasn't so damn sexy when he was being an asshole. Mostly.

His lips twitched. "You would deliberately provoke me?"

She arched a brow. "You say that like I'm supposed to be afraid of the big bad kitty." Okay that might be pushing it, but as far as Cian was concerned, she was powerful enough to curse him. Any sorceress with that kind of strength wouldn't be easily bullied, not even by a gargoyle using his size and proximity to intimidate her.

Elena would be proud of her.

"You and I can talk privately or we can involve your lovely companion. I believe her name is Leah."

"You leave her the hell out of this."

"So the sorceress has claws too."

"And I swear to the gods you'll feel every one of them if you so much as lay a whisker on her."

"There you go with those threats again."

"Threats?" She smirked, feeling the power build in her palm.

Cian hissed and jumped away from her. He glanced down before shooting her an accusing look. "You burned a hole in my pants."

Shrugging, she took advantage of the space to backtrack toward the slot machines. "It barely had a chance to smolder." She scanned the vicinity, looking for a way to ditch him.

Her phone beeped and she dug it out, accessing the text message from Leah.

Already next door. Will catch up with u later.

Now why didn't it surprise her that Leah had already grown bored? At least Cian couldn't use her—

He snatched the phone out of her hand.

"Give that back."

"No." He pocketed her phone, thankfully without looking at the screen.

Arrogant pain in the ass. She didn't say it out loud, though, aware he watched her closely. She wouldn't give him the satisfaction of knowing how easily he riled her up.

She glanced at the closest slot machine, doing her best to

pretend he wasn't standing less than a foot away. Turning her back to him at least proved she wasn't concerned with an attack from behind. What didn't work was keeping her breaths even when he crowded against her, casually setting a hand on her hip.

"You're boring me, gargoyle."

He nuzzled her neck. "Is that all I'm doing?"

"Now that you mention it, I'm feeling a little nauseous."

His hand tracked across her abdomen, sliding inside her jacket to graze her exposed midriff. "Want me to kiss it better?"

The image of him on his knees in front of her, pressing slow, open-mouthed kisses to her stomach, was going to stay with her for a good long time.

She shrugged him off and dug the token out of her pocket. It seemed like a smarter move than tipping her head to give him access to her neck.

Dropping the token into the machine, she pulled down the bar, wondering what the hell she was supposed to do now. Magic was definitely out. It was a wonder she hadn't set him on fire a moment ago. Better not to push her luck.

So intent on figuring a way out of her mess without being seduced by the gargoyle again, she was slow to notice the same images line up, one after the other, in front of her.

She wasn't sure which of them was more stunned when lights flashed and an alarm sounded.

Cian released her, and the second the confetti started raining down on them—it would be her luck to win something cool when she wouldn't be around to claim it—she bolted.

Realizing someone had won a grand prize of some kind, people immediately moved closer to see. Emma plowed right through them, not even looking to see how close Cian was.

By the time she hit the lobby, drawing way too much attention to herself in the process, she risked a glance. He wasn't behind her.

She didn't have time to take comfort in that, but breathed a little easier when she made it outside without him catching up to her. Her lead was marginal at best though.

Darting across the street, and nearly getting mowed down by a tour bus in the process, she ducked around a corner. A group of tourists emerged from one of the souvenir shops that were a dime a dozen on the strip, and she sprinted right past them, slowing only when she turned another corner.

Chest heaving, she leaned against the wall to catch her breath. She reached into her bag for her phone, then remembered Cian had confiscated it.

Damn it, how long could this go on? Would he spend the next decade—or worse, the next century—tracking her? She shuddered at the thought. She just couldn't decide if it was the bad kind or the really naughty kind.

Footsteps pounded the pavement.

Cian.

There really wouldn't be any outrunning him, would there? It was a small miracle she'd pulled it off the first time. Magic it was then.

Drawing a steadying breath, she pushed away from the wall and waited for him.

Two men rounded the corner, surprising her. She stepped to the side, waiting for them to pass her.

They didn't.

She glimpsed a Fae glyph branded on the shorter guy's neck. Shit. Avalon help Elena if she'd just dragged Emma into yet another mess.

She cocked her head, waiting.

"You need to come with us," the taller of the two ordered, and the faint tang of a smoldering fire hit her nose.

Dragon.

Yeah, her sister was so dead.

Chapter Six

He was going to kill her. Slowly. Painfully. It was the least the sorceress deserved for the stunt she'd pulled back in the casino.

Cian shook what he hoped was the last of the paper out of his hair. He wouldn't be a bit surprised to start coughing it up given how much of the stuff had been dumped on him. His head was still ringing from the alarms, and even escaping outside hadn't helped.

After nearly tearing through his skin to break free, the cat still rode dangerously close to the surface. It had taken everything inside him to hold on to his human form when the damn sky had started falling.

And to top it all off, he felt like an ass for being taken by surprise by little flakes of colored paper.

Catching the barest hint of his mate's scent, he crossed the street. He could deny his connection to her all he wanted, but it didn't stop him from responding like she was his. With nothing but time over the last four weeks to feed his fury over what she'd done, he hadn't be prepared for how quickly his anger had faded.

Relief had hit first that she hadn't been harmed by another without him there to protect her, followed by a need so sharp and deep it nearly cleaved him in two.

And the way she responded to him...

He'd begun to wonder if what happened between them before her escape had been an act on her part. The way she had all but melted in his arms inside the casino suggested that wasn't the case.

Either she'd been caught up in her own spell or she was truly attracted to him. The latter gave him a small slice of satisfaction, even as it undermined his determination to break the hold she had on him.

Up ahead, two men hurried down a side street, one of their scents distinctly dragon and blending with Emma's.

It couldn't be a coincidence they were headed in the same direction, not when he had a feeling trouble routinely followed the sorceress.

Cian's heart picked up speed even as he forced himself to slow down to avoid their notice.

Emma was close.

The pair disappeared around the corner ahead, and Cian increased his pace. Instead of following the men, he leaped onto the blue truck parked in front of the building on the corner, then higher onto the slanted roof.

Staying low, he made his way to the edge that looked down on the space between buildings where Emma stood watching the two men.

"You need to come with us."

Definitely trouble. And if either of them took another step closer, he'd enjoy tearing their throats out.

Emma shook her head. "Sorry, but I was raised not to go anywhere with strangers."

The men exchanged glances, as if silently deciding who would make the first move.

A tease of power curled across the back of his neck, similar to what he'd felt in the casino right before she nearly unmanned him. From his position on the roof, he could see Emma's palm behind her back and the flicker of a flame.

"I'm in no mood for games," one of the men snarled.

What was she waiting for? She'd lost the element of surprise—if she'd even had it to begin with—and from the way the taller one was sizing her up, the dragon was going to strike.

Cian unzipped his pants, stripping out of them and his shirt before sending one more curious glance at his mate.

"We know who you are, Emma of Lamorak."

The fire in her palm faltered, nearly extinguishing. "I'm afraid you have me confused with my sister."

Sister?

The shorter one—a Fae—shook his head. "We know why you wear the jacket, Emma."

Her face gave nothing away, but the first scent of real fear from her unleashed the cat inside him.

His vision sharpened as he gave himself over to the change. Bones and muscles realigned, and he pawed the ground, his senses magnified in his animal form.

"I'd rather you just came along quietly." This from the dragon. "But my friend here doesn't mind getting rough with his females."

Cian leaped down onto a stack of industrial-sized containers, then to the ground below, planting himself between the pair and Emma.

He didn't have to worry about the dragon. Only one with a death wish would shift within a thousand miles of any human population. Cian was pushing it himself, but at a distance, humans could talk themselves into thinking he was no more than a large dog. He shuddered at the thought.

The dragon, however, would have every huntress on his ass if he was that stupid. The Fae posed more of a threat at the moment. The Fae race was the oldest of all immortals, and their ability to fabricate complex glamours that could trick someone into seeing something that wasn't there made them highly unpredictable.

"If you come willingly, we won't have to turn your furry friend into a throw rug."

Cian snarled, and only the brush of Emma's fingers along his back eased the feral instinct to kill the threat to his mate.

"You can certainly try, but I think it's only fair to warn you that he's one of the Guard."

The dragon instantly took a step back, his head bowing in a show of respect. He shot his friend an apologetic look. "I didn't sign up for tangling with one of Arthur's gargoyles, bro."

The Fae shrugged. "If you're out, that leaves more of the reward for me." He fixed his attention on Emma. "The Guard is obsolete."

Cian tracked the Fae's progress as he circled to the left. The dragon, although he hadn't left, retreated to the far sidewalk.

"Reward for what?" Emma demanded, the soothing touch of her fingers betraying none of her anxiousness.

"For delivering you to Gareth."

Emma's fingers dug into his fur, and Cian snarled at the Fae.

Unconcerned, he circled them, his movements slow, precise. A burst of fire shot past Cian, and the Fae shimmered and vanished.

Not the Fae, Cian realized, lunging to intercept the

immortal who had used a glamour to mask his attack from the opposite direction.

Steel struck cement as the Fae slashed with the sword he'd also concealed. Snapping his jaws, Cian caught only the Fae's clothing, and the rip of fabric only fueled his need to sink his teeth into him.

He didn't have a clue who Gareth was, or if Emma deserved the price he had apparently put on her head. It didn't change the fact that Cian would be the one walking away with the female.

The Fae's sword whistled past his head, and he waited as the immortal drew his arm back for another strike, then sprang forward. He hit the bastard in the chest, taking him to the ground.

Pain ripped across Cian's side, and the Fae kicked him off. Blood trickled on the ground, but he'd already pivoted for another strike.

Another burst of fire from Emma caught the Fae's shoulder. His expression turned murderous and he flung his arm out, backhanding her.

Red sliced across the cat's vision as Cian surrendered entirely to the cat.

His mate hit the ground, but then so did the Fae as she swept her leg out and knocked his feet out from beneath him.

Cian lunged forward, closing his teeth around the bastard's throat.

"Wait." Emma touched his back. "If you kill him, then he can't tell Gareth that he won't get what he wants."

He glanced at the Fae, his jaws itching to snap shut. The Fae had struck his mate—that alone was enough of a reason to finish him.

"I won't have blood spilled over me if I can help it. Please," she added when he still hadn't eased his grip.

The Fae twitched beneath him, and Cian couldn't help it—he tightened his hold.

"He promises to get lost. Right?" She directed the last part to the Fae, then cocked her head. "Was that blink for yes or no?"

The Fae blinked rapidly.

"I'm pretty sure that's a yes."

It could have been a blood promise and he still wouldn't have let go. Sighing, Emma picked up the sword the Fae had dropped and tossed it behind her. "Does that make you feel any better?"

He'd feel better if the Fae was dead and no longer a threat to her, but finally relaxed his jaw. Backing away slowly, he prayed for the Fae to make just one wrong move, even a hint of one.

The other immortal scrambled to his feet, his hand going to his injured throat. The flow of blood had unfortunately started to slow. In a couple of hours there wouldn't be any sign of the wound at all.

Slowly, the Fae backtracked. Instead of watching his retreat, Cian watched his mate. She'd seen through the Fae's glamour, and by following her gaze he wouldn't be fooled again.

Only when the Fae joined the dragon and they disappeared around the corner did he sit back and stare at the sorceress. She stared right back at him, waiting.

"Are you planning on sitting there until someone spots you and calls animal control? I'll bet the zoo would love to put you on display. You could roll around on your back and hiss at the tourists."

He snorted, but didn't move, unsure if he could trust himself not to pursue the Fae.

"Don't even think about it."

Hearing Emma's voice, he realized he'd already taken a few steps in that direction.

"I don't need your death on my conscience."

He growled, insulted that she didn't believe he could have protected her.

"Please." She rolled her eyes as if understanding him completely. "I'm not talking about the Fae taking you out."

Take him out where?

She studied something above his head. "It's the sorcerer that he's working for I'm worried about. As much as you've been a colossal thorn in my side, I have no desire to see your furry ass skinned and declawed."

Had he been a man he might have missed the subtle undercurrent of...fear?

She was afraid for him? She'd used her magic to curse him because of something Tristan had said, and now she worried what would happen to him?

"Whoa." She took a hasty step back. "You're naked."

Somewhere between his confusion and pleasure that she didn't want his furry ass hurt—he was rather fond of it himself—he'd seamlessly shifted back.

"Who is Gareth?"

She averted her gaze—because she didn't want to answer or because he wasn't wearing anything? He dismissed the latter immediately. She'd seen him without any clothing on before.

Her gaze drifted to his chest before darting away again, only to return a heartbeat later. "You're hurt."

He shrugged, the pain in his side barely noticeable compared to what a glimpse of that barely veiled hunger in her eyes did to him. Except it was more than that, wasn't it? Like what he'd sensed during their night together—something deeper. Something that had him moving closer.

I wasn't expecting that. Wasn't expecting you.

"Don't," she whispered.

He frowned.

"Make up your mind gargoyle. Hate me or..." She trailed off.

"Or," he prompted.

"Whatever. We don't have time for this now. It won't be the zoo that gets called about a bleeding, naked man in the streets. How good are you at pretending you're wasted?"

"Wasted? As in pretending to be garbage?"

She smiled. "No. Drunk. Landing in the drunk tank for a few hours is probably better than being arrested under suspicion of some other crime." She let out a breath.

She did that a lot. Released a breath and ran her finger across her cheek to catch any loose strands of hair before tucking them back behind her ear. The movement drew his attention to the soft curve of her jaw where he'd pressed his lips before. She had moaned then, a soft hiss of pleasure that gave him all kinds of dangerous thoughts.

Like how good it would feel to run his tongue up to her mouth, or lower, down her throat and stopping when he reached between her legs.

"Where are your clothes?" A flush of color brightened her cheeks, just like the night in his room when he'd stripped out of his shirt.

"A sorceress with a guilty conscience and uncomfortable with nudity."

"Not all nudity. Just yours."

She smacked his hand away before he could curl his fingers around the delicate shell of her ear. "Stop that."

"I'm not making you nervous, am I?"

"The dragon and Fae made me nervous. You just annoy me."

At the mention of the Fae, he growled, his animal half itching beneath his skin.

"Oh no." She jabbed her finger into his chest. "You go all cat on me now and I'll turn you into a carnival toy."

"Truly?"

Her chin dropped only a fraction. "Without even blinking."

He laughed. "Make up your mind, sorceress. Hate me or..." He trailed off intentionally as she had moments ago.

"Where. Are. Your. Clothes?"

"On the roof."

She followed his gaze, holding out her hands. Her eyes brightened from gray to a brilliant purple, the pulse of power like the drag of a hot feather up his spine.

"Here." She turned and thrust something into his arms.

He didn't need to look down to know it was his clothes. He caught her hand before she could back up. Watching her face closely, he teased his thumb across the inside of her wrist.

Her gaze snapped to his, and he lifted her hand to his face, his eyes sliding shut. The cat stretched its claws in pure pleasure at her touch, making it even harder to get the words out.

"I can't live like this, Emma. I can't keeping fighting myself. Can't keep wanting you this much when it's nothing more than a lie." He turned his face into her palm. "You need to make it stop. Please."

The rough plea twisted Emma's heart. "I can't." Damn Elena for putting her in this position.

Music blared between them, and he dropped her hand.

Seeing the confusion on his face, she slipped her ringing phone out of his pocket. "It's just my cell. Get dressed."

Facing the sidewalk and hopefully keeping herself between Cian and anyone who strolled by, she glanced at the call display.

Elena. About freaking time.

She didn't even waste time with hello as she answered. "You've really done it this time, you know that?"

"Thank Avalon you're okay."

Emma frowned, hearing the relief in Elena's voice. Okay, she hadn't been expecting that.

"You're in trouble, Em."

She slid a sidelong glance to the gargoyle tugging on his pants. "You don't know the half of it."

"It's Gareth."

"I know. Two of his lackeys were just here."

"Are you okay?"

Another glance at the man behind her. "Mostly."

Cian cocked his head. "Emma?" He held up his shirt. "What happened to this?"

The expensive shirt he'd been wearing was full of holes. Damn.

She ignored his question. "You and I need to talk."

Elena blew out a breath, and she felt her unease increase. Even neck deep in trouble, Elena rarely sounded worried. "I know. Meet me at Leah's. I'll be there in less than an hour. I've already reserved Leah a suite at the Bellagio for a couple nights to keep her out of harm's way."

"You sure she'll be safe enough? I can—"

"She'll be fine. You need to worry about yourself for once, Em. Gareth isn't screwing around this time."

"You think he'll try again."

"We both knew your last refusal to honor the alliance would only buy you a little more time." Static echoed over the line. "Is the gargoyle still with you?"

"How did—"

"Keep him with you, Em. You need him."

"What I need is for you to undo—"

A dial tone echoed in her ear. Elena had hung up on her.

Oh no. She punched in Elena's number, cursing under her breath when the call went right to voicemail. Taking a deep breath, she slipped the phone into her bag and faced Cian.

"You're in trouble, aren't you?"

"You could at least pretend to sound surprised."

"My brother mentioned that he and Sorcha crossed paths with more than one immortal eager to find you."

Big surprise there. "Would you believe me if I said it was just one big misunderstanding?"

"Which part? Other immortals hunting you or this Gareth sending people to bring you to him?"

Refusing to think about Gareth right now—the determined sorcerer was an even bigger pain in her ass than Cian—she started for the sidewalk. "It's not safe to stay here." It wouldn't be safe for her anywhere if Gareth was intent on finding her. She'd foolishly hoped he and her father had found someone else to use in their power play against the other houses. Apparently not.

"You're not going anywhere until you undo this." He motioned to the space between them like there was literally something binding them together.

Thinking about what Elena had said, she shook her head. "You think those kinds of castings can be done anywhere?" She didn't mention she wouldn't be doing any of them.

His eyes narrowed briefly. Too bad the suspicious look he threw at her didn't make him any less sexy. His ruined shirt wasn't helping either with all those fine abdominal muscles on display.

"Are you trying to get me alone, sorceress?"

"I'm trying to give you what you want. Unless you've changed your mind."

He closed the gap between them, and her attention slipped to his mouth before she could stop herself. "How do I know I can trust you?"

"You don't, but what other choice do you have?"

"Aside from locking you up and throwing away the key?"

"Yeah, because that worked so well for you the first time."

He smiled, but the feral edge to it warned her that the cat was still very close to the surface.

She turned away, half surprised he made no move to stop her, but the second her back was turned, he jerked her against him.

"One more thing." His lips brushed her ear, and she called on every molecule of self-preservation she possessed to ignore the heat that seeped into her back. "You owe me a new shirt."

She owed him more than that, or Elena did anyway. Nodding, she stepped away from him the moment he released her.

Leah's loft was only a few blocks from the Strip, but walking next to Cian, feeling his gaze burning into her the whole way, made it feel more like half a continent away.

"You count cards."

Startled after walking for so long in silence, she only nodded. She couldn't see the point in lying about it. After today they wouldn't be crossing paths. At least she intended to do everything possible to avoid him in the future.

"Why not magic?"

She shrugged. "I'm good with numbers." Better than she was with magic, as evidenced by the shredded shirt he wore.

He gave her that look again, like she didn't make sense to him. He gestured to her jacket. "Why are you wearing that?"

"I have a fondness for outerwear?"

"It's hot and sunny and you are dressed for a crisp autumn night."

"It's comfortable." And it wasn't the heat from the sun that was threatening to set her skin on fire. Every time he looked at her, as if remembering the feel of her beneath his mouth, another nerve ending went up in flames.

"Then what did the Fae mean when he said he knew why you wore it?"

"I have a scar." It wasn't a lie, but the scar that crisscrossed the ivy tracing that ran the length of her spine didn't make her feel half as self-conscious as knowing other immortals could assess her strength with a single glance.

Cian planted himself in her path. "Someone hurt you?"

She knew her sister's spell was to blame for the possessive anger in his voice, but for a moment she pretended he really meant it. No one but Leah and Elena had ever been protective of her, and thinking of the cat ready to do the guilty party damage touched a place deep inside her.

Not real, she finally reminded herself. "It was just a childhood prank gone wrong." That's what her father had insisted even though the ten-year-old sorceress responsible had damn well meant it.

The weak deserve to be put down. Two centuries later and the bitch's words still echoed in Emma's head.

He caught her hand, the tenderness in his eyes stopping her dead in her tracks. "For such a powerful sorceress, you don't hide your pain very well."

Her throat grew tight, but before she could imagine what it would be like to have him soothe those old hurts, she ducked around him. "Careful, Sylvester. You're already too attached to me as it is."

"Sylvester?"

"You know. Bugs Bunny. Daffy Duck. Sylvester." Maybe he hadn't spent enough time watching television to know who she was talking about.

"The cat that always fails to catch his prey?" He scoffed at the comparison, apparently having seen an episode or two.

"If it makes you feel any better, it's not really Sylvester's fault that Tweety is so clever."

"Tweety can fly. I'd say that gives him a certain advantage."

She mulled that over before coming back with, "Dragons can fly too. Does that mean you've never bested one?"

"Too many to count." The response was pure, arrogant male.

"So what—Sylvester isn't predatory enough, is that it?" She shrugged. "I suppose you're right. You *are* a hunter. Elmer Fudd is a much better fit."

"Fudd? He couldn't catch a rabbit if someone duct-taped one to his ass."

Emma hid her smile. "Leah's loft is just around the corner."

She heard him mutter something under his breath about Fudd being an embarrassment to all hunters everywhere. She dug her key out of her bag, acutely aware of Cian giving her only enough room to breathe as she unlocked the door.

Inside the door, he came to a standstill next to her, and she followed his gaze to the floor-to-ceiling mural on the opposite wall.

"The battle of Camlann," he whispered. Eyes locked on the mural, he walked down the few stairs into the sunken main floor.

He reached a hand out, running his fingers across the likeness of King Arthur in the middle of the battle, the red dragon insignia on his shield making him impossible to miss. Around him, knights and gargoyles protected his back, fighting Mordred's army though they were outnumbered ten to one.

Despite the brutal violence of the piece, the agony on the faces of the wounded, their injuries splashed across the battlefield in bold strokes of red and black, there was something so hauntingly beautiful about it that captured Emma's attention every time she walked past.

Above the battle, the goddess Rhiannon looked down from the sky, forbidden to interfere and change the events that had been set in motion thousands of years before. Camelot rose in the far distance, its ivory stone walls gleaming in the setting sun, a beacon of peace amidst such savagery.

"Who painted this?"

"Leah. The woman with me at the casino."

He glanced back at her. "The human? How could a mortal

have painted this, as if she'd been there?"

"My sister and I told her about it."

He traced the outline of Excalibur, then his arm dropped back to his side. He fell silent after that, never taking his eyes off the mural.

"How did you survive?" She knew so few did. The vicious battle raged long after both Arthur and Mordred had fallen. And of those who'd lived, so few made it out of Camelot when Morgana had laid siege to the kingdom.

"I would have died on the battlefield that day if not for Constantine. When Arthur...when we lost our king, some of us became ruled by our animal halves. Near the end I had been almost cleaved in half by a Fae, and although I could barely move, I felt no pain. I had no chance of besting him. I knew it, but I was prepared to die if it meant I might at least take the Fae with me."

Emma's pulse picked up speed even though he obviously hadn't lost the fight or he wouldn't be standing in the room with her now.

"Constantine had other ideas," Cian continued. "He finished the Fae off and dragged me off the battlefield. When I had healed, along with a few other of the Guard and a handful of Arthur's Knights, we tracked the gargoyles who'd betrayed us. They'd left an opening in the ranks that Mordred's men had slipped through to reach Arthur that day. We left none alive."

He turned away from the mural finally, and although the battle had taken place centuries ago, the instinct to comfort him, to soothe away the pain still imprinted on his face, had her closing the distance between them.

"I'm sorry."

"It happened a long time ago."

"For an immortal that can still feel like yesterday."

He glanced at the mural again. Not wanting the images to make him relive any more of the death and bloodshed from such a dark time, she laced her fingers though his and tugged him in the opposite direction.

"This way. You're still bleeding." It was a lame excuse for holding his hand, and if the gargoyle saw right through it, it didn't stop him from tightening his fingers around hers.

He trailed her into the small bathroom, waiting while she dug through cupboards for a bandage.

"I don't think this is going to cut it." The bandage in her hand wouldn't cover much more than a paper cut.

"It's fine."

"We should at least wash away the blood." She rinsed off a cloth and, pushing aside his shirt, gently dabbed at the dried blood.

Cian sucked in a breath.

"Sorry. It's still bleeding quite a bit. Leah must have something in the master bathroom upstairs."

His hand closed over hers. "I'll live."

She stared at his hand, so much larger and stronger than hers. She'd never had a choice but to acknowledge she wasn't as powerful as most of her race, but something about the way she felt when Cian was this close made her feel strong, important.

"Will it take long to heal?"

"Not long at all if I went to stone."

"So why don't you?"

The look he gave her spoke volumes. What gargoyle would ever willingly turn in the company of the one they'd believed kept them trapped that way?

"Guess I can't blame you there. I..." Nothing she could say would ever make up for it, would it?

Cian stared at her, waiting.

"I'm going to check the master bathroom."

He followed her, pausing at the bottom of the stairs, his hands locked around the railing.

If Elena didn't get here soon she might end up doing something stupid, like telling the gargoyle the truth. She might have already if she wasn't worried that the spell that left him enchanted by her wouldn't offer Elena the same protection.

She couldn't imagine him physically hurting her twin, but if he got aggressive, there was no way to guarantee Elena wouldn't retaliate. Staring at her reflection in the upstairs bathroom, she shook her head. "Just who are you trying to protect here?"

Her phone rang, and she drew in a relieved breath when she saw Elena's name. "Where are you?"

"Get out of there, Emma. Now! There are more than I thought. More on the way. They know about Leah."

"More on the way?"

"Bounty hunters. Treasure seekers. Anyone looking to build an alliance with Gareth's house. Meet me—"

A growl erupted through the phone.

"Elena?"

The sound of an explosion. "...bastard..."

"Elena!"

"Get out of there, Em." Another explosion. Elena screamed, and the phone went dead.

Fuck. Fuck. Fuck.

She tried redialing. Busy signal.

Darting out of the bathroom, she collided with Cian in the hall.

"What's wrong?"

What in Avalon wasn't wrong? First Cian showing up at the casino, then the pair who followed her and now Elena in trouble. She tried to tell herself to stay calm. Elena was much too powerful to be easily taken by anyone.

Without looking at Cian, she hit redial again. "My sister. I think they have her." She had to force the words out, torn between fury and fear.

Someone answered. "Elena?"

"This wouldn't happen to be pretty little Emma, would it?"

Just hearing Urien's voice was like an oily snake slithering across her skin. Her stomach churned in revulsion at the thought of Gareth's right-hand guy, a lethal Fae, getting anywhere near Elena.

"If you touch one hair on her head—"

"You'll what? Give me a first-degree burn? Why don't you save the threats for people capable of executing them, love."

The only thing more frustrating than knowing Urien had Elena was knowing the bastard was right. Her casting ability didn't come close to matching Urien's strength even on her best day.

"I'll be seeing you soon, love. And don't worry—I'll take real good care of Elena."

"You son of a bitch."

He hung up before she finished getting it all out.

"We need to go."

Urien would take Elena to Gareth's stronghold. Which meant if Emma had even a prayer of reaching Elena, she needed to catch up with them before they reached his land.

How she'd accomplish that when his home bordered on Avalon's barren region was another colossal obstacle altogether. The terrain was nothing short of treacherous.

"Wait just a minute."

Ignoring him, she rushed down the stairs. Cian beat her to the bottom by leaping over the rail and landing at her feet. "Wait."

"There's no time."

"Make time. Undo your spell, sorceress."

She glared at him. "They have my sister."

"Not my problem."

She shoved past him, but he caught her arm and jerked her around. "You will not go running off before you fix this."

"I told you, there's nothing—"

Glass rained down from the skylight above. There wasn't time to raise an arm to shield her face before Cian flattened her against the wall, shielding her body with his own.

Across the room, wood splintered as Leah's front door was smashed in and two men, both dressed in combat camouflage, joined the third who had dropped through the skylight to land on the stairs above them.

Three-to-one odds weren't so bad.

Two more burst through the oversize window Leah used to access the fire escape.

Cian spun around, keeping her pinned between his back and the wall. He didn't seemed concerned with the fact she couldn't breathe, and if she wasn't just a little bit scared—okay a lot scared that he'd put himself between her and Gareth's mercenaries—she might have been a little annoyed.

"Do something," Cian hissed, more cat than man.

"I'm open to suggestions.

"You're the almighty sorceress. Magic might be a good place to start."

"About that..." she began.

An arrow sliced across her peripheral vision, but Cian snatched it out of the air before it sank into his arm.

Emma's mouth fell open. Everyone knew cats had damn good reflexes, but not that good, and from the way Cian was staring at the arrow, he was equally stunned.

Taking a breath, she lifted her palm, focusing her energy on the fire building in her palm. The closest guy lunged at Cian, and the two collided.

When another mercenary moved in on Cian, she released the purple fireball. It nailed the guy in the chest, sending him into the mural across the room. The impact knocked him out cold.

Holy shit. Emma stared at her palm. Purple? She closed and opened her fist. "Did you see that?" She didn't wait for Cian's response before she focused on the guy with the crossbow above them.

He leaped over the side like Cian had earlier. Behind Mr. Crossbow another mercenary snarled and dropped to the ground, his clothes shredding as he shifted into a wolf in a shower of color that wasn't nearly as impressive as Cian's.

Keeping her gaze trained on Mr. Crossbow, she released another burst of fire. Even before the flame left her hand, she knew it was a dud. A few feet in front of her target, the fireball popped and fizzled out like a faulty firework.

Cian flipped the first guy over his shoulder and stepped back toward her. "Impressive," he drawled, tracking Mr. Crossbow.

"Last I checked I neutralized one of them." Who was still out cold on the floor. "How about you?"

"I won't leave you unprotected."

Great, so either his misplaced sense of protectiveness was going to get him killed or her unpredictable magic would.

"No one else needs to get hurt." Though Mr. Crossbow spoke to Emma, he glanced at Cian.

"If I come with you, you'll leave him here? Unharmed?"

Cian shook his head. "No." It was more of a feral growl than anything close to English.

"I will not be responsible for anything else happening to you." His injuries from the Fae were enough to feel guilty about.

"Maybe that should have occurred to you before you turned me into a two-ton roof ornament." The accusation in his voice fueled her frustration and she shoved away from him.

"You think I'm using this as an excuse to get out of helping you?"

"It is rather convenient."

"They have my sister."

"Maybe."

Son of a bitch. "And what are they?" She jerked her head at the men staring at them like she and Cian were some kind of reality T.V. train wreck. "Just for show?"

Cian stared at Mr. Crossbow. "She goes, I go."

Her frustration level shot off the chart. "Unbelievable. I'm trying to help you, you stubborn, overbearing excuse for a gargoyle."

"You can help me by undoing your spell."

Did the man have any understanding of time and place? "I either hit you too hard with the toilet tank cover or not hard enough."

"And you wonder why I'm having trouble trusting you?"

"Enough!" Mr. Crossbow's voice boomed over theirs, cutting them off. He fired another arrow, which Cian easily intercepted.

"Fuck," he snapped, and Emma glanced down at his thigh where a second arrow was lodged. He curled his fingers around it, then lost his grip.

"Cian?"

Eyes glazed over, he leaned into her.

"What did you do to him?"

Cian staggered, knocking them both into the wall. Looping her arms around his waist, she struggled in vain to keep him on his feet, ending up half underneath him when his knees buckled and they hit the floor.

Mr. Crossbow notched another arrow, this one aimed at the back of Cian's skull. "Are you going to cooperate now?"

Chapter Seven

She was gone.

It was the first thought to register as Cian slowly awakened. That, and what the fuck had they hit him with?

Every inch of his skull throbbed like he'd been struck with a blacksmith's sledgehammer. He cracked open an eye, and even the sliver of light that penetrated made him curse. After a few seconds of wondering if he'd empty his stomach all over himself—since he wasn't even sure he could roll to his side—he tried again.

The pain wasn't so bad this time, only seven out of ten instead of eleven. He blinked a few times, bringing the plain white ceiling and overhead lights into focus. Where was he?

Taking stock of any other injuries besides his head, he realized the floor beneath him was hard and cold, but his head was propped up on something much softer, warmer.

Bracing against another wave of nausea, he turned his head. Even before he saw her, he recognized Emma's jacket. Her eyes were closed, her head tipped to the side, her lips parted by shallow breaths. The steady rise and fall of her chest helped quiet the cat.

They hadn't hurt her, not enough to stop her from resting his head in her lap anyway.

Yet another contradiction. She'd been so angry with him at her friend's home, her eyes turning purple like she was contemplating hitting him with one of her fireballs, and here she was next to him.

The female made his head hurt, and that was without whatever toxin they'd used to subdue him. Most immortals metabolized poison too quickly to be more than temporarily weakened by them.

Still feeling the effects, he stayed where he was and looked around the room. The slate gray walls and two metal chairs offered no indication of where they were.

Maybe he should have let Briana come along. There's no way she would have let him waltz right after Emma without some kind of plan—one that didn't involve landing smack in the middle of the sorceress's mess. Did she make it her life's mission to infuriate other immortals or did it just come naturally?

Emma sighed in her sleep, her brows drawing together.

"Hey."

She jolted awake, her palm coming up as if to fire off another burst of magic. He caught her hand, lacing his fingers through hers. "Easy."

"You're okay."

If he didn't know better, he'd swear she was worried about him. "Cats have nine lives, remember."

"They wouldn't tell me what was in the arrow." Her expression turned critical. "How's your leg?"

Before he realized her intentions, she gently probed his thigh.

His breath hissed out at the wave of pleasure that raced across his skin.

She pulled her hand back. “Sorry.”

“Don’t be. For a moment I forgot how much my head hurt.”

“Is it bad?”

He smiled, uncomfortable with the guilt he swore he heard in her voice. “About a hundred times worse than the concussion you gave me.”

“I’d apologize for that, but you did have it coming.”

“I had it coming?”

“Forget it,” she snapped in that female tone that clearly said she wasn’t about to forget anything.

“Oh, no.” He sat up, regretting the fast movement the moment his stomach plummeted halfway to his knees. He couldn’t have held back his groan if he tried, sucking in a breath so he didn’t embarrass himself any further. It was bad enough he hadn’t been able to prevent their current predicament without adding insult to injury.

“Touch my leg.”

“What?”

“Please.” He didn’t wait, but set her hand on his thigh, hoping the world would stop spinning so fast.

“Better?” she asked a moment later.

It would be if he could find a way to get her hand a few inches higher. That would make it all better. He wisely kept that to himself though. Her soft gray eyes seemed to spark with purple, and if he made her angry, the last place he wanted her hand was anywhere below his waist.

Not that he had to worry about that for long when she tugged her hand free and swept her thumb across his bottom lip.

“Your lip was cut when they dumped you on the floor.”

"Feels fine now." Very, very fine.

"Good." The way she was staring at his mouth was going to land both of them in more trouble sooner or later. And damn, he hoped it was sooner.

He dropped his head and his cheek grazed hers. Almost there.

The sound of a lock disengaging echoed in the room, and the door swung open.

They both turned to look at the man—a wolf gargoyle if Cian's senses weren't off from the poison—who ducked beneath the frame to get inside and closed the door behind him.

Someone on the other side engaged the lock.

"Emma? Are you okay? I just heard you were here."

Cian was on his feet before the other gargoyle took a single step in her direction.

"He's a friend." Emma winced and tried to stand, and Cian turned to help her.

"If he hurt you," the wolf began, glaring at Cian.

"I'm fine, Dillon. Unless you count my legs falling asleep under him."

Ignoring the newcomer, Cian kept her close. "You could have left me wherever they dropped me."

"And have to listen to you complain about another head trauma?"

Head trauma? Ah, the concussion.

She shrugged. "The floor was cold." She didn't give him a chance to challenge her motivations further before focusing on her friend. "Tell me you can get your brother to let us out of here."

Cian frowned. "Brother?"

"Dillon's brother owns the casino we're in, the Wolf's Den."

"Did he catch you counting cards?"

She scoffed. "Counting cards is not illegal. It's just...frowned upon."

Dillion snorted at that, then shook his head. "Sorry, Emma. He's sort of barred me from the penthouse."

She crossed her arms. "What did you do this time?"

Cian shot a glance first at Emma, then Dillion. "Does she normally sound that scary?"

"Tell me," she pressed, ignoring Cian.

"It had nothing to do with slipping a human any ambrosia if that's what you're thinking." His shoulders slumped. "It's my mother."

Mother, sister, ex-girlfriend and some crazy blackjack dealer he'd seduced a week ago, Cian decided after listening to the guy pour his heart out to Emma for at least fifteen minutes.

He stopped trying to keep track after the last time Emma's fierce glance promised bodily harm if he tried to interrupt one more time. Apparently Dillon's problems with females—numerous problems—were more important than the fact that they were still locked up.

And not only was Emma showing little interest in using her magic to get them out of there, but he was as protective of her as ever. Dillon could cry all he wanted, but if he tried to catch another glimpse of Emma's cleavage, Cian was putting his fist in the wolf's face.

He didn't realize his claws had burst through his skin until Emma scowled at him, in particular at the grating sound they made against the chair he sat on.

Shooting Cian a curious look, Dillon nodded toward the door. "I should go. I'll try to talk to my brother again, but the reward for delivering you to Gareth is enough to tempt even the most loyal, Emma."

"I know."

"I'll be back as soon as I can." He knocked on the door and just before it opened, Cian gave thought to making a move.

"We'd make it down the hall. Maybe," Emma said, reading his mind in that eerie way of hers. "But we'd never make it past the Korrigans blocking access to the main casino floor."

"Maybe you're content to sit and wait for your sorcerer friend to arrive, but I'm not." The four walls were starting to feel too close, crowding him. He knew it was in his mind, but after being trapped for a century, he didn't want to spend a minute here longer than he had to.

"What should I do? Pretend to be sick and you'll hide behind the door and jump out when someone comes to check on me?"

He perked up. "You don't think they'd be expecting that?"

She rolled her eyes. "You haven't caught up on much television yet, have you?"

"I fail to see what one has to do with the other. Fine, you want to stay, then undo your spell and I'll leave you to your fate, sorceress."

"It would be that easy for you, wouldn't it?"

Right now the only easy thing to do would be haul her close and kiss her until neither of them could see straight. The thought of leaving her here, leaving her anywhere, made the cat snarl at the back of his mind. He was counting on the spell being reversed to fix that.

She sighed. "It's more complicated than it seems."

"Uncomplicate it," he gritted out.

"I can't... Wait." She held up a hand when he started to tell her he was done waiting. "How good are your tracking skills? And don't give me that arrogant look as though I should just assume you're a skilled hunter."

"So I should just tell you that I'm a skilled hunter?"

"But not the best. Only the best can track through Avalon's barren region."

He snorted. "It's not being able to track someone through that region that makes someone the best. It's catching them."

"And I suppose you've accomplished such a feat," she mocked.

"Was there ever any doubt?"

At his admission, Emma's gaze turned calculating, and he instinctively knew she'd set him up. He just didn't know what for.

"You want to be free of me? Then you'll help me track my sister before she's taken to Gareth."

He burst out laughing, then stopped when Emma didn't join him.

"You're serious?" He didn't wait for her to respond, the determined look on her face saying it all. "I'd sooner pledge my soul to Morgana."

"Not even she can undo another sorceress's spell."

Red slashed across his vision. "I wasn't wrong about you at all, was I? You truly are a manipulative bitch who doesn't care who she hurts."

She flinched, but didn't back down. "Do we have a deal or not?"

He stalked away from her, whirling back around a moment later. "Do you enjoy playing with peoples' lives?"

"No more than you enjoyed playing with mine when you refused to release me."

He glared at her, saying nothing.

"Not so high and mighty now, are we?"

The door across the room opened, and Dillon popped his head inside. "My brother wants to talk to you."

Cian lowered his voice. "Stay close to me." He didn't like being backed into a corner—and Emma had him good and trapped—but leaving without her wasn't an option.

If it took playing along until a way out of their current situation presented itself, he'd bide his time. Later he could be annoyed with himself for not anticipating such a move on Emma's part. Right now he needed to stay focused so he could take advantage of any opportunity that presented itself—and Dillon was staring at Emma's chest again.

The wolf glanced at him, then quickly looked anywhere in the room but at Emma.

"Why is the sorcerer after you to begin with?" Cian asked as they stepped into the hall. Immediately they were flanked by two men in camouflage gear, with two more taking up the rear. "Did you turn him to stone too? Maybe make him fall in love with a troll?"

Emma ignored him. Thankfully Dillon didn't. "She's been promised to Gareth."

Cian stopped, snarling when one of their armed escorts shoved him to get him walking again. "What do you mean *promised*?" Because it damn well couldn't mean what he thought it did. His animal half considered Emma his and spell or not the man wasn't much further behind.

"You been living in a cave, dude?"

"Something like that." He shot Emma a dark look, but she was too busy staring at the floor.

"They did do something to you, didn't they?" It was the only thing that explained why she hadn't used her magic against the men surrounding them. It made sense that a group as organized as their escorts appeared to be would have measures in place to contain powerful magic.

It couldn't be a handcuff or chain. Something more discreet maybe. Although she hadn't complained back in the room. And why was that? She'd made numerous references to the chain nulling her magic weeks ago.

When the doors at the end of the hall parted and they were ushered inside a room only a little larger than a closet, a wave of uncertainty rolled through him. Only when the doors closed, sealing them inside, did he back up, snarling.

He knew there was a name for the box they rode in, had seen them on television. Being familiar with what it was didn't stop the cat from rising to the surface.

"He's fine."

Hardly, which was why it took him a moment to notice the arrow pointed at his stomach.

Emma stepped between the two closest guards and faced Cian. The box jolted and he growled, searching the ceiling for its weakest point.

"Look at me." She caught his face between her palms, forcing him to meet her gaze. "We're safe."

He watched the words form on her lips. They just didn't make any sense when his heart felt like it was going to pound straight through his chest.

And then all he knew was sweet softness. Achingly sweet as Emma slanted her mouth across his. Everything but his mate faded into the background, the icy panic freezing his blood replaced by a rush of heat.

Her body pressed up against him, fitting snug, chest to

thighs. So snug there was no way she would have missed how hard he was. Her fingers speared the ends of his hair and he groaned into her mouth.

Moments ago he'd been afraid she was going to get hurt if he didn't keep a grip on his panic. Now he feared she would pull away before he got enough of her. He just didn't know when that would be.

Emma wasn't sure if she'd pushed him against the wall to get him farther away from the arrow or so she could lean into him completely.

The longer she stood there, losing her mind to a kiss that started out as a means of distracting him, the more she suspected it was the latter. She would have given anything for another minute of feeling his lips slide across hers, drugging her in slow, possessive degrees.

She vaguely registered the chime of a bell as the elevator doors opened, and she tried to ease back. He curved his palm around her nape, keeping her right where she was. Objecting would mean pulling away and pretending she wanted to stop, and they'd barely gotten started.

Though one more hot stroke of his tongue and she might be done. Right there. In front of the men who'd gone speechless around them, she could collapse in a quivering pile of sheer want.

"Em," he whispered against her lips, and the equilibrium keeping her on her feet was shot all to hell.

"Really, Emma? A cat?" Dillon scoffed in disgust, then spun around, smashing his fist into the closest guard's face.

Cian jerked her to the side, knocking one guard off-balance while he nailed the one directly behind her in the jaw.

Something hit the floor. The crossbow. With little room to maneuver, the last guard still standing could only try pushing her out of the way to reach Cian. Light flared between them and he howled, cupping his crotch.

"Go," Dillon yelled, gripping the guard's head and yanking it down to meet his knee. He shoved Emma out of the elevator, then delivered a solid kick to the third guy's stomach and hit the panel.

Catching Cian's hand, she pulled him into the hall as the doors scrolled closed, leaving them in the penthouse's marble foyer. Off to the immediate right was a lounge area and beyond that an elaborate dining room. Everything was painted in caramel and deep chocolate browns, the furniture leather and solid looking.

She'd bet Dillon's brother was a bachelor.

"We need to find the stairs." They would have to be close to the elevator, wouldn't they?

Cian left her side, venturing deeper into the penthouse.

"Hey," she hissed.

A door on the right swung open and she instantly recognized Mr. Crossbow. Cian, having the element of surprise, caught the guy around the neck and tossed him—head first—into the door. Bones crunched on impact.

She didn't get the chance to see if the guy was still conscious. Cian slammed the door shut, then grabbed her hand, keeping her close as he led her down a hall on the left.

"Looking for a closet to hide in?" she quipped.

"Well, I was thinking about finding a bed to crawl under, but I like your idea better." He stopped. "Do you hear that?"

A thump echoed from farther down the hall. Cian headed in the same direction.

"You won't be able to track my sister if we get caught." Judging by the murderous look he shot her, he didn't appreciate the reminder.

Guilt swirled in her stomach like curdled milk. As frustrating as he was, she hated having to force him to help her. She'd almost told him the truth downstairs, but if he knew her sister was the one who'd cursed him, he might decide to let Gareth have them, at least until he saw reason. By then both her and Elena's fates could be sealed.

Right now the gargoyle was her best shot at getting to Elena, and whether he liked it or not he needed her too. Another thump, followed by a grunt.

The room opened up ahead of them and a cage, like something from an ultimate fighting match, dominated the center of the room. Two men—one with the same red dragon tattoo as Cian's on his back—were locked together, angling for a hold that would take the other to the floor.

Cian released her hand and strolled into the room like he owned the place.

A century in stone really had caused some brain damage.

The guy with the tattoo noticed them first. He frowned, and the slip in concentration cost him. He went down hard, his opponent wrapping his legs around him like a human pretzel.

Cian stopped and tucked his hands in his pockets. Giving up on trying to blend into the background, Emma joined him in time to see the pinned guy get his arm free and do some kind of move she had to tip her head to follow.

His opponent tapped his shoulder and the pair parted.

Hopping out of the ring, his mouth split into a wide grin. "Cian." He slapped him on the back in greeting. "I didn't know you'd been freed. Man, it is great to see you."

Maybe things were finally looking up. If this guy knew Cian, maybe he stood a chance of talking Dillon's brother into releasing them.

The guy fixed his gaze on Emma and his grin widened. "Tell me you're not with the cat and I'll lay my heart out right this second."

She didn't get the chance to respond before Cian stepped close, the low growl of warning unmistakable.

He laughed. "So it's like that, is it? Easy, friend, I have no interest in tempting your female." He winked at Emma before motioning them to the bar tucked near the window offering a panoramic view of the Strip. "Tell me you caught up with the sorceress bitch that left you in stone."

She felt Cian's glance at her, and her cheeks heated.

"Nevermind." He handed her and Cian a shot glass. "So what are you doing in Vegas?" He paused, glass halfway to his lips. "No one told me you were on your way up actually." He glanced back the way she and Cian had come. "Vincent?"

Emma winced. "If he's about six-foot, blond and wicked with a crossbow, he's catching a catnap in the bathroom."

"Why..." He turned the full impact of those wolf eyes on her as though sizing her up for the first time. "Your name isn't Emma, is it?"

She nodded. "And you're Dillon's brother, Mac."

"Shit. And you're the gargoyle who was brought in with her?" He directed the last part to Cian. "What, tangling with a sorceress wasn't enough for you, you had to go and provoke a sorcerer by taking his intended as a mate?" He rubbed a hand down his face. "How did you two wind up here alone anyway?"

"We were looking for a closet actually."

Cian snorted and Mac gave her a strange look. "Forget I

asked. You can't stay here though."

Footsteps echoed down the hall, and they turned as another joined them. "You threaten to feed some of your people to Morgana's trolls again? They're all running around..."

The newcomer stopped when he spotted them.

Mac grinned. "Yeah, Lucan. It's him."

Tall, blond and with eyes so dark they were almost entirely black, he greeted Cian with the same enthusiasm as Mac had.

Emma cocked her head. "Lucan? As in the wraith who marked Kennedy?"

Like the gargoyle clans, the former Knights of the Round Table had also been punished by Rhiannon. Even those most loyal to Arthur hadn't escaped the goddess's wrath. She'd permanently bound them to her, hiring them out to the highest bidder for engagements that usually involved assassinating other immortals.

Kennedy had mentioned that ignoring or prolonging the completion of a job literally drove a wraith insane. It was only a matter of time before the unspeakable pain they suffered for defying the goddess turned into a vicious bloodlust that eventually overtook them, consuming them until they completed their assignment.

As if that wasn't enough, they were forced to drink blood to survive, and the venom in their phantom claws made even the most fearless immortal nervous to be in the same room with them.

Cian arched a brow. "I left you alone with Sorcha and Kennedy for an hour."

She shrugged. "Girls talk. She doesn't hold it against you, you know." She doubted passing that along would ease the guilt she'd momentarily glimpsed in the former knight's eyes.

"Tristan still does."

"Give him some time." Cian turned back to Mac. "What did you mean about not staying here?"

Mac shot him an apologetic look and motioned for them to follow. "I mean some of Gareth's pals are on their way to get her. My team was just the middleman."

"They might have my sister, Elena, with them."

Mac shook his head. "I don't think so. My contact mentioned that his group was splitting up and only he and two others were coming for you."

Cian frowned, looking at Emma. "Why would this sorcerer only send three men to collect you?"

"He's arrogant?" she offered, though that wasn't the whole truth.

Mac ran his fingers along the top edge of a painting. "Admitting I released you won't be good for business." He shoved the key into the wall and another set of doors scrolled open to reveal another elevator. "You get them out of here and I'll deal with Gareth's people."

Lucan nodded, slipping into the elevator ahead of them.

"Watch your back, Cian. Gareth doesn't play nice, and he won't stop coming until he gets what he's after."

The doors closed and Cian went perfectly still. Jaw tight and gaze fixed straight ahead, he sought out Emma's hand, linking their fingers. If Lucan noticed the elevator bothered Cian, he never let on.

When the doors finally opened, they were in an underground parking garage.

"You can take my car." Lucan dug the keys out of his pocket, and she grabbed them a second before Cian.

Snippets of Lucan's life flashed across her mind in hyper

speed. In a few heartbeats she understood why Arthur had made him one of his knights. Even hired out as a mercenary, she knew with a touch of his keys that he still believed in honor, loyalty and Camelot.

Cian stopped, watching her expectantly, his eyes locked on the keys.

As if. “Maybe if people hadn’t been still using horses for personal transportation a hundred years ago I’d consider letting you drive.”

Cian scowled at her when she unlocked the car and slid behind the wheel. She lowered the window as he dropped into the passenger seat.

Lucan leaned down. “Tell Tristan to call on me if he needs anything.”

“I will.”

“And everyone else is alright? Cale? Briana?” The slight emphasis he put on Briana made Emma sit up a little straighter.

“Everyone is well,” Cian answered, still staring at the keys she’d shoved in the ignition.

When the wraith felt her studying him curiously, he ducked his head. Cian either didn’t notice or wasn’t surprised by Lucan asking about Briana. It didn’t take an oracle to see Lucan had been hoping for something a little more.

“Her computer password is Lucan, you know,” she offered. At least her laptop password had been, before she’d changed it to Pendragons when she’d given it to Cian.

Cian frowned. “How would you know that?”

She shrugged and started the car. “Buckle up.”

Lucan gave her a small nod, his expression guarded as he stepped back. Putting the car in reverse, she slid Cian a sidelong glance, anticipating the same tension he'd exhibited in the elevator.

"If you go cat on me, you're sitting in the back."

"Tristan let me drive his car a few times. I enjoyed it immensely."

A few times? And he'd been ready to snatch the keys right out of Lucan's hand?

Luckily, she'd been faster. With Cian driving she might not have made it out alive.

Chapter Eight

He wasn't going to make it out of the car alive.

Cian gripped the door handle as she took another corner like a maniac, prepared to dive out of the car if it came to that. He was fairly certain he'd rather take his chances with oncoming traffic.

"Could you perhaps—"

She passed another vehicle at speeds the human race should not be traveling.

"—slow down?" he finished.

Tristan had driven him around the city with the top down on his BMW, and he'd reveled in reaching speeds faster than his animal half could run. Right now though, he was praying for it all to stop.

Instead of slowing down, the car picked up speed.

He slammed his eyes shut, only to crack one open at the last second. The car opposite them seemed oblivious to Emma bearing down on it, and made a left-hand turn.

Cian's breath hissed out as she swerved to clear it. Did she not know how to use the brake?

"Sure, I do," she said, and he realized he'd spoken aloud. "We're just on a really tight schedule."

"Tell me again why we didn't just cross into Avalon at

Mac's?"

Conversation was good. By talking he could pretend they weren't one more corner from colliding head on with another car. Immortals could survive almost anything, but beheading wasn't one of them, and he'd be damned if tucking themselves into a metal box on wheels and traveling at speeds as fast as the gods wasn't tempting fate.

"We need supplies first." She weaved around two more cars, coming so close to the second one he was sure he heard the scrape of paint.

"I'm not scaring you, am I?" She glanced at him.

He pointed at the road. "Look that way."

The crazy female grinned at him. "So I bet this would really freak you out." She let go of the steering wheel.

If he could have bent over and kissed his ass goodbye, he would have.

"Relax, you can look now. See?"

"Two hands," he growled, looking through the fingers on one hand. "Put them both on the wheel."

"If you say so."

He really didn't like the way she said that.

Without warning, she wrenched the steering wheel in her hand, sending the car into a spin across oncoming traffic and down a narrow lane. After taking one more corner—during which he'd vow the car drove on only two wheels—she slammed on the brake.

It took him a full minute to pry his claws from the seat.

She turned to stare out the back window. He followed her gaze, certain a dragon must have been after them.

"That red SUV has been following us almost since we left the Wolf's Den. I wanted to ditch it just to be on the safe side."

"Oh good. So there's a reason you nearly killed us."

"Hey, I've taken defensive driving courses."

"Maybe you wouldn't need whatever that is if you didn't have people after you all the time."

"Contrary to popular belief—" *his* popular belief according to the look she gave him, "—that's not the norm for me."

"You've had people after you as long as I've known you."

She reversed onto the street, heading in the opposite direction of the red VUS or USV or whatever she'd called it. "You don't count. Neither does Gareth."

Just the mention of the sorcerer looking for his mate enraged the cat.

"Do you love him?" He didn't know why he asked or why it even mattered when his feelings for Emma weren't real. Probably had something to do with the paralyzing fear that had been coursing through him since she'd gotten behind the wheel.

"No. His interest in me—marrying me—is only about aligning our families."

"Are you sure about that?"

"What other reason would there be?"

He faced her. "You really don't see it, do you?"

Suspicious, her eyes narrowed. "See what?"

"How beautiful you are."

She snorted. "That's the spell talking, remember?"

Was it? He wasn't so sure anymore. The spell might fabricate the instinctive connection he felt to her, the depth of it, but anyone could see how stunning her eyes were and her smile...

"You're staring at me." Her cheeks flushed a pretty shade of pink.

"You're blushing."

"Am not." She glanced over her shoulder before passing the car in front of them. He grinned, unsure if she was driving slower, or if he'd momentarily forgotten her driving was more terrifying than a legion of Morgana's bloodthirsty trolls.

Definitely the latter, he decided another minute later, cursing as she pressed her foot right to the floor.

"Pull over."

"Now?"

He nodded, struggling to keep still on the seat. "I need out of the car, Emma." He wasn't sure how long they'd been driving but it was enough he needed to be able to move more than a few inches in any direction.

"I think I saw a sign for a rest stop another mile or two ahead."

Or maybe five. Or ten. That's how long it seemed before she pulled off the main road and parked near a sheltered picnic table. She hadn't brought the car to a complete stop before he threw open the door and climbed out.

He dragged in a deep breath, getting as much space between him and the parked car as he could.

"Cian?"

"I'll be back in a minute." Jumping over a ditch, he slipped into the trees. The deeper into the woods he moved, the easier it was to pretend the world around him hadn't changed so drastically. Out here he didn't need to worry about cars or elevators, or misunderstanding what someone was saying.

And he didn't need to worry about the sorcerer who wanted Emma.

He slashed out at the closest tree, his claws slicing through the bark. Even the scent of the trees and surrounding wildlife wasn't enough to mask Emma's scent.

"Cian?"

He closed his eyes. Twigs snapped beneath her feet as she took a few tentative steps toward him.

"Are you okay?"

"You're good at that, you know."

"At what?"

"Sounding like you care."

"Look, I know that you think I hate you or something—"

"I don't know what to think. You're so full of contradictions. One minute you're trying to manipulate me and the next you seem worried about me when I've done nothing to deserve your concern. Why is that, Emma?"

A soft smile curved her lips. "I'll let you know when I figure it out myself."

He dropped his head, breathing in her scent. He wasn't sure what answer he'd been expecting, but that wasn't it. The female was leading him in circles. He had a better chance of catching and chewing on his own tail than figuring her out. And trying to understand such a confusing, spellbinding creature was slowly driving him out of his mind.

Everything inside him said she was his, and the only thing that stopped him from accepting it was the knowledge it was all based on magic. But the cat didn't care. It grew increasingly agitated that Cian fought his instinct, and it was only a matter of time before the cat won.

"I have a new deal for you, sorceress."

Her gaze turned wary.

"If you want me to track your sister, then you need to do

something for me. You need to act like you're my mate."

"What?"

"Continuing to fight the spell distracts me, and if I'm distracted, then I might miss something."

She shifted on her feet. "And you won't be as distracted if…" She trailed off the moment his lips grazed her cheek.

"If I'm not pretending I don't want you."

Her eyes drifted shut. "So what is it exactly that you want from me?"

He studied her mouth, remembering the feel of it beneath his. "Nothing we haven't already done."

"We don't have a lot of time."

His nose bumped hers, and then he was a breath away from sinking into her lips. "If you want my full cooperation, you'll make time." He nipped her bottom lip, then pulled it slowly between his. "Do we have a deal or not?"

His gut told him she'd give in, but if he was wrong and she refused, he didn't know how he'd make himself let go.

"I don't think it's a good idea."

He was pretty sure it was the best idea he'd ever had. And when he gripped her hips and tugged her flush against him, he was convinced of it. "I'm not talking about forever."

The cat vehemently disagreed with him.

"Just until we find my sister."

"Mmmm," he managed, eager to get to the part where he put his mouth all over her. Her increasing arousal was like a teasing stroke along his cock, making him achingly hard, and any second she was going to notice.

"Okay—"

He didn't give her a chance to finish. He opened his mouth

over hers, claiming as much of her as he could. They hadn't truly finished the kiss in the elevator and he meant to make up for that starting right now.

Emma sighed, and the sound entranced him. He slid his tongue across hers, rubbing soft and slow and nearly frying his brain in the process.

Sweet Avalon.

Sinking his hand into her hair, he tipped her face up just a little more. Another breathy little sigh passed her lips, and he groaned in response.

There was no way she could know what hearing that did to him. She might not be so quick to respond to him if she realized every sound of pleasure brought him one step closer to pushing her up against the tree.

She twined her arms around his neck, and he took instant advantage by rocking his hard length against her. Her nails dragged across his nape, and she moaned into his mouth. Any plan to savor her, to linger over her mouth before moving down her throat to her breasts and the hard nipples he could feel right through her bra, went up in flames.

Between one rough breath and the next, he walked her backward. Her mouth moved in perfect rhythm with his, like they could take each other all the way in as long as they didn't stop.

He pushed her jacket down over her shoulders, giving him more room to tug her shirt up. His fingers skimmed across her belly, not stopping until he cupped her breast.

This time he was ready for that breathy little sound she made, and deepened the kiss. She arched into him, her lace-covered breast filling his palm to perfection. He shoved her shirt up, along with her bra, then bent to flick his tongue across the dark pink tip.

She watched him from beneath heavy lids, her eyes dark with need. The kind he was more than capable of satisfying. Dipping down, he closed his lips over her nipple, pulling her into his mouth.

Her soft cry echoed through the trees, and she ran her hand through his hair, holding him to her. With a teasing drag of his teeth, he released her, giving her only a second to catch her breath before returning to her mouth.

He didn't even try to pretend he wasn't half out of his mind for her. Which likely explained why he didn't remember slipping his hand between them. He rotated his palm in lazy circles, feeling her tremble.

"Is it coming back to you now?"

"Um..." She trapped her bottom lip between her teeth.

Unsnapping the button on her pants, he eased his hand inside, sucking in a sharp breath at how hot and damp she was.

"What about now?" He ran his fingers along her slick part, circling her clit, but not touching it just yet. He wanted her a little wilder, wanted her clinging to him tighter, needing him as much as he needed her.

"I think so," she murmured.

"You don't sound certain." He pushed against her snug opening. "Does this help?" He thrust a finger inside her, pumping in and out.

She tucked her face against his throat. "Yes."

"Is that yes, you remember? Or, yes, more?"

She answered him by easing her legs a little wider, and he took the opportunity to drag the moisture up to her clit, swirling over the swollen knot.

Her breath caught, and he knew she was close to release.

Too close. He softened his touch so the pad of his finger barely brushed her.

"Cian."

"You still haven't answered the question." He let his hand fall back.

"I don't know." Frustration flashed in her eyes.

That made two of them. He should have known better than to assume he could make sense to either of them when he couldn't think of anything but making it good for her. The more aroused she became, the more satisfied they'd both be when she found release. Watching her ride the peak, feeling her clench tight around his fingers and knowing he gave her that pleasure would be almost as good as sinking his cock inside her.

And if he was really lucky—and he planned on it—he was going to get both.

"Please." Emma caught Cian's hand, guiding it back between her legs. Need pulsed through her in long, scorching waves. She laced her fingers through his as they brushed her sex.

"Please, what?"

Impatient, she rolled her hips. Just another stroke of his fingers… "Touch me."

He stared at their joined hands. "I like watching you touch yourself." The intensity in his gaze made her even hotter, and she couldn't help but run his fingers down her sex to her opening.

"I need to feel you inside me." She watched his eyes darken, and then he pumped two fingers inside her. Already so aroused, the slick invasion made her feel impossibly full, and she squeezed her thighs together.

"Fuck." He groaned against her mouth, his tongue pushing as hard and deep as his fingers. Between thrusts, he abandoned slow and soft in favor of fast and hard as he plunged his fingers inside her.

She rocked up on the balls of her feet. So, so close. His thumb brushed her clit, rubbing in harder circles.

"Oh." She sank her teeth into her bottom lip, giving herself over to the climax that streamed through her.

Cian's mouth slid across hers in a long, lingering sweep of lips and tongue.

I'm not talking about forever, he'd said, but with the way he kissed, she might have agreed to it. Agreed to anything if it meant she could feel this way for the rest of her life.

Cian made a sound against her lips, low and rough and like he was feeling the same thing she was. Except, for him, it wasn't real.

There wasn't time to dwell on that, though, as he continued to work his fingers inside her, until she moaned long and deep, eager to feel his hard length sinking into her.

Without warning he stepped away from her, but his hands weren't at his zipper where she wanted them.

He stared at the forest behind her. "Another car just pulled up."

Trying not to give in to paranoia, she shrugged. "It's a rest stop."

"Stay here." And then he was gone, moving so quickly and silently through the trees, she might have imagined that he'd just had her pinned to the tree trunk.

A very solid tree trunk, she realized, now that he wasn't distracting her from the rough bark she felt right through her jacket. She fixed her pants, self-conscious now that she was alone.

Had she made a mistake agreeing to his terms? But what choice had there really been? She'd never find Elena on her own.

She'd be lying to herself if she denied sex with Cian would be any kind of hardship. And it wasn't as if she was about to fall in love with him. In another couple of days—tops—he'd be out of her life for good. As long as she kept reminding herself of that, she'd be fine.

God, what was wrong with her? Why the hell was she even thinking about falling insanely head over heels when he didn't even like her?

"There are only three of them."

She jumped at the sound of Cian's voice. She hadn't expected him to come around the tree from the opposite direction.

"Only?" She narrowed her eyes. "Why are you looking at me like that?"

Without answering, he took her hand, pulling her deeper into the forest. "They'll be able to track us. Running isn't an option."

"You want to fight them?" She wasn't sure whether to admire his bravery or punch him for being so stupid.

"There are two of us."

Was he serious? Either the poison the arrow had been dipped in had scrambled his brain, or he'd forgotten how things had gone down at Leah's. "I can't."

He glanced over her shoulder, frowning, but not slowing down. He didn't ask for an explanation, but she knew he was waiting for one.

She let out a breath. If they were caught again, it wouldn't matter if she continued to let him believe the worst about her. She wouldn't get another opportunity to get away. Gareth would somehow make sure of it.

"It was the cuff, wasn't it?" Cian stopped, his gaze scanning the trees. "Its power is still affecting your magic, isn't it?"

Hearing the guilt in his voice, she frowned. "My problems with magic are not your fault." Not even close.

He didn't look convinced. "Take off your jacket." For once she didn't hesitate. If he needed to see how few tracings she possessed to recognize the truth, that was more than fine with her.

She slipped out of it and handed it to him.

"Now climb that tree."

"What?"

He turned her around. "Up. We don't have a lot of time."

"Cian—"

"Later."

Giving in, she used the closest branch to pull herself up, helped along by a firm push on her butt from Cian.

She paused to look down at him. "What about you?"

He dragged his shirt over his head. "I'm going to try and throw them off your scent." He finished stripping and tossed his clothes and shoes into a far bush. "You need to get higher. Now."

In the last glimpse she caught of him between thickening branches, he was shifting into his cat form. Giving her one last quick look, he picked up her jacket in his mouth and disappeared into the trees.

A short while later—maybe longer—she heard a wolf howl in the distance. If the wolves thought they were tracking her and Cian, would they give themselves away like that?

Either they thought they knew Cian's location and wanted him to know they were close, or one was closing in on him and called to the others for help cornering him.

If the slobbering mutts laid a paw on him, she'd—

A large black cat leaped into the tree above her. "You scared the crap out of me. Again," she hissed.

Two piercing green eyes stared through the tree at her.

Wait. Green eyes? Cian's were blue—which meant the sleek predator an arm's length away wasn't Cian at all.

For a heartbeat she thought about pretending she didn't know the difference, and then the cat showed off a mouthful of sharp teeth. Her scent, she realized. The cat could tell by her scent that she was afraid.

Just not enough to forget how to defend herself entirely.

With a wave of her hand, the branch beneath the cat snapped and he scrambled to a higher limb, giving her only a marginal head start down the tree. Even then, she hit the ground only a second before the gargoyle.

Heart pounding, she met the animal's eyes, refusing to show any fear. She focused on pulling energy into her palm, letting the fire build. "You've got about five seconds to go find a mouse to play with or you're gonna lose your tail."

Tension coiled along the cat's back a moment before he sprang forward. She released the fire, relieved when it didn't fizzle out this time. Unfortunately, the cat darted to the side at the last second and the fireball slammed into the ground. Her next one grazed the cat's right flank.

Growling, the animal lowered its head, one leap away from ripping her apart. She raised her hand for one final strike.

Inches from her face, a black blur collided with the

attacking cat.

Cian.

Silky fur whispered across her hand before they hit the ground, ripping into each other as they rolled through the underbrush. Leaves, moss and branches were kicked up as the cats slashed with their claws, their massive jaws sinking into each other's fur.

Even from a distance she could hear the sound of flesh tearing, each animal determined to come out the victor. Since both of them were black, it was almost impossible to tell which cat was Cian. The occasional glimpse of their eyes wasn't enough to tell them apart for more than a few seconds at the time.

The pair slammed into a tree before one sank its teeth into the other's neck. The wounded one reared up, shaking the other off its back, hard enough to knock it into a slab of moss-covered rock.

The cat swayed on its feet, dazed, but instead of facing off against its opponent, it lunged for her.

Definitely not Cian.

The ground rushed up to meet her as she dove to the side to escape being pinned beneath the animal. But she wasn't fast enough to avoid the claws that ripped across her back.

Crying out, she dug her feet into the earth for traction and heaved herself up. She only made it as far as her knees before Cian knocked her out of the way. She landed on her back, sucking in a sharp breath at the pain that flared between her shoulder blades.

Twice more she barely got out of the way of the battling animals. Her back came up against a tree as the two broke apart, circling each other.

A wolf howled, closer now than before. If another gargoyle caught up with them with Cian already wounded...

Refusing to finish that thought, she made it to her feet as they went on the attack once more, this time ending with one trapped beneath the other. Another gut-churning sound of flesh tearing and then the one on top snapped its head around. Victory gleamed in the cat's green eyes.

"No!"

Her neck tingled as another burst of energy burned hot in her palm. She shot it outward, the purple flame nailing the cat head-on and knocking it away from Cian. It still wasn't enough to keep the animal from staggering back to its feet.

Her skin blistered beneath the heat of another fireball, but she held on, letting it build.

If Cian was—

Gareth's gargoyle disappeared beneath a flash of black fur. She looked away as Cian finished him off.

"Cian?"

The cat didn't lift its head until another wolf howled, then he turned and limped toward her. Even though his sleek coat masked some of his injuries, in other places she could see right through the ripped flesh to the bone.

He didn't give her the opportunity to look him over before nudging her into a run. It didn't take long for him to trail her and twice she had to slow down, afraid if she kept going he would drop behind her.

They finally burst through the trees, and she spotted a house on the other side of the field. "There." They must have circled back closer to the interstate.

She looked over her shoulder just as Cian collapsed. Tripping over a tree root to reach him, she dropped to her knees.

"You can't stop now. I know you cats are big on napping, but now sure as hell isn't the time."

His eyes drifted shut.

"Cian. Get up or so help me—"

The wolves' howls were growing closer. "If you thought a century as a statue was bad, just wait and see what I do if you don't haul your furry ass to that house."

He cracked open one eye.

"Cian, please. Get up. I need you to get up."

The cat's limbs shook as he pulled himself up, and he leaned against her as if catching his breath.

"We need to go."

He refused to move until she started ahead of him.

"Are you always so stubborn, or do I just bring it out in you?" She started across the field and Cian thankfully stayed with her the whole time.

Just as they reached the house, she saw two wolves break through the trees on the opposite end of the field.

"Inside." She scrambled up the stairs as Cian used the last of his strength to break the door down.

If anyone was home, they were about to have the crap scared out of them by a ravaged cat. When no one called out or came tearing through the house at the sound of the door being smashed in, she sent out a silent prayer of gratitude. The last thing she needed to deal with was innocent humans caught in the crossfire.

Emma scanned the kitchen. "Mirror. I need a mirror." The bigger the better. Moving through the kitchen, she turned left down the hall. "In here."

"Em."

At the weak sound of Cian's voice, she spun from the full-length mirror attached to the sliding shower doors in the bathroom.

She sucked in a breath so hard her lungs hurt. Cian leaned in the doorway in his human form, coated in blood from the claw and teeth marks covering eighty percent of his body.

Sweet Avalon.

"Is it truly that bad?" The words had barely left his mouth and his knees buckled.

Between the arm she threw around his waist and the vanity, he managed to hold himself up.

"I'm all right."

She would have told him he was insane if she could speak past the thick lump wedged in her throat. *Don't think about it.*

Slamming the bathroom door shut, she flipped the lock even though it wouldn't do a damn bit of good in keeping the wolves out.

She faced the mirror and pressed her palms to the glass. Almost immediately, she felt the surface warm.

"I thought only Fae could enchant a mirror?"

She ignored the question, trying to focus. She hadn't attempted to forge her own portal between worlds since she was a child, and at the time she'd used a pond. Water was easier to manipulate than mirrors, and that was without the added pressure of two gargoyles closing in on them.

The hard surface rippled beneath her palm, and her reflection shimmered twice before finally giving way to a shadowed place on the other side. Too dark to be Elena's lair.

"They're here," Cian whispered.

Out of time, she snagged the two towels off the rack next to the mirror, along with the pair of sweatpants draped across the top of the laundry basket, then slipped one arm around Cian's waist.

"They won't be able to follow us."

"How unfortunate." Cian winced as he leaned against her.

Like walking through cobwebs, the veil slipped over them as they emerged on the other side. In an instant, the tease of ancient magic washed over her.

"This isn't...we're not..." Cian stared at the enormous cavern where they were standing.

Her stomach turned inside out. "In the catacombs? Yeah."

Shit.

Chapter Nine

The catacombs.

The weight of defeat nearly crushed Emma's shoulders. She should have tried something else, shouldn't have assumed she had the control it took to cross the veil and end up exactly where she wanted to.

But the catacombs? Gareth's dungeon would have been preferable. Hell, even Morgana's dungeon would have been better.

"I've always been a fan of the scenic route myself." Cian shifted too much weight to her, and she barely got him to the ground without losing her grip altogether. It was a miracle he'd been able to stand long enough to cross over.

She grabbed one of the towels she'd brought with them and pressed it to his ravaged neck.

"Breathe, Emma. It's not as bad as it looks."

"You haven't seen it." And it wasn't as bad as it looked. It was worse.

"We were just in front of a mirror."

She applied as much pressure as she could, even when he cursed under his breath. "Yeah, and how many Cians did you see?"

He tried for a smile. "Good point."

Blood quickly soaked through the towel, and she grabbed the second one. “It’s not slowing down fast enough. You need to shift back.” She knew his animal form was more resilient than his human one.

“No.”

“Could you not be such a stubborn ass just this once?”

“And miss an opportunity for you to scold me?”

“Scolding is just the tip of the iceberg, pal.”

He shifted and sucked in a sharp breath. “I’ll go to stone the second I shift.”

“Which is exactly what your body needs.” It would take longer for his body to heal if he didn’t, and the thought of watching him suffer until then left her shaking inside.

“You’re holding your breath again.”

She snatched up the first towel again, covering another wound on his side that left his ribs exposed. “You have too many injuries.”

“I won’t leave you unprotected.”

“Forgetting the fact that I’ve done a fine job of protecting myself before you came along, how exactly do you plan to defend me like this? Bleed all over my assailant?”

He started to shake his head, his face pale. “Sometimes you talk too quickly.”

“Don’t change the subject.”

“Can’t do it. If you leave—”

“I won’t.” Careful of his wounds, she took his face in her hands. “I swear to you that I’ll stay right here the whole time.”

He nodded as if he finally understood. “Because you need me to find your sister.”

Because she wasn’t sure she could walk away from him,

not with her heart intact. Admitting that, though, would make it real, so she brushed her lips across his. "You need to heal."

His hand came up to cup the back of her head as he deepened the kiss, not pulling away until they were both breathing hard. He rubbed the base of her throat. "It suits you."

"What does?"

"Your ivy."

She frowned, touching her throat. He was in worse shape than she thought if he was hallucinating. Her only tracings encircled her wrists and ran down her spine.

At Cian's hesitant nod, she eased away from him, giving him plenty of room to shift. She glanced down at the blood staining her hands, and her stomach twisted. It was her fault he'd been hurt. She should have found a way to keep him out of this.

A furry head butted her hand and she bit her lip at the sight of such a stunning creature wounded and hurting. Because of her. She crouched down, and Cian rubbed his face against hers, turning to stone when he'd barely begun to warm her skin.

She lingered beside him until some of the pressure on her chest eased, then she stood and faced the cavern.

Okay. Now what?

The white blossoms on the vine-covered walls glowed, giving off more than enough light to see from one end of the cavern to the other, but wandering too far wasn't an option. Only the oldest Fae could successfully navigate the maze-like tunnels of Avalon's catacombs, and only those with something of interest to one of the elders could barter for a charm that would lead to the nearest exit.

Stories of even the bravest immortals losing their way in

the catacombs had populated bedtime stories for centuries. Emma wasn't interested in becoming a story children were told to keep them from exploring the catacombs.

She'd be fine as long as she didn't venture too far along any of the tunnels leading away from the cavern, not until Cian finished healing anyway. Then they'd find a way out. Somehow. She'd never heard of a way to cross the veil in the catacombs, the ancient magic here making a stable gateway bridging Avalon and the human realm impossible.

The catacombs had been created by the Fae during the first Campaign, when the gods had turned on each other, and not even Titania, queen of the Fae, had been able to prevent the gods from turning their sanctuary into a battlefield.

Thousands of immortals had been recruited, coerced or forced to fight the gods' war, making them little more than expendable pawns. Everyone else had become victims caught in the crossfire. Some believed the catacombs had absorbed so much magic throughout the war that the endless labyrinth was actually alive, that it deliberately prevented the immortals who lost their way from ever finding their way out.

Right now that was Emma's least favorite tale. Even if she doubted a tunnel could suddenly close itself off as if it had never been there, she wasn't sure she wanted to risk it. Crazier things had happened than the catacombs coming alive.

Like a gargoyle believing she was his mate.

Sometimes magic just sucked.

Warmth washed over Cian as the cold stone broke away from his body, the chunks disintegrating before they hit the ground. He moved into a crouch at the unfamiliar surroundings, then his memories caught up with him. He turned and spotted Emma immediately, curled up on her side, something rolled up beneath her head to keep it off the ground.

Fully healed, he padded over to her, nudging her first with his head and then, after shifting back to his human form, with his hand. Her lashes didn't so much as flutter with either attempt. The female slept like the dead, leaving her vulnerable to who knew how many creatures that could have crept up on her.

Expecting her to wake any moment, he stretched out beside her. It seemed like a much better use of his time than prowling around the cavern until she woke up. He wasn't sure how long he'd been stationary, but he'd guessed at least half a day considering how extensive his injuries had been.

The sorceress could have used whatever magic had landed them in the catacombs to get as far away from him as possible. Instead, she'd kept her word and remained with him. Because of her sister? Or another reason altogether?

He had barely been able to think straight when they'd crossed the veil. Every inch of his body felt like he'd been run through by a dozen swords straight out of the blacksmith's fires. Every inch except his heart, because when Emma had vowed to stay with him, he'd believed her.

Believed that it didn't have anything to do with her sister and everything to do with what was between them. And it wouldn't have been half as terrifying if, for a moment, he hadn't wanted his feelings for her to be real and not based on a spell.

He brushed a stray curl behind her ear the way he'd witnessed her do a hundred times. He'd lied to her in the forest. He wanted more from her than sex. He wanted to know more about her, like how she'd learned to count cards, or what had possessed her to stop and help a woman on crutches when she'd been hell bent on getting away from him.

He wanted to know why she really favored her leather jacket when the scar he'd felt on her back wasn't big enough to be disfiguring in any way, and why she would risk her life by sharing the existence of immortals and Avalon with a human.

Most of all he wanted to know how a sorceress could snatch away a hundred years of his life so thoughtlessly, but be so fiercely protective of her family. The female was a walking contradiction, and the more time he spent with her, the more he wondered if there could be any truth to what she'd said.

"Would you believe me if I said it was all just one big misunderstanding?"

Emma's lashes fluttered finally, and she nestled closer to him with a sleepy sigh.

"Hi."

Her eyes snapped open, and she rocked to a sitting position, bumping her head against his chin. "Sorry." She looked him over carefully, her gaze lingering on his neck as she ran her finger over his healed skin. "You're okay."

He didn't think she was looking for confirmation, but he nodded anyway. A smile exploded across her face, and she launched herself in his arms, her grip almost strangling him.

"Missed me, did you?"

He regretted speaking at all when she released him, ducking her head in that self-conscious way that made her seem so vulnerable. He caught her around the waist before she could squirm out of reach altogether.

"What? Did you suddenly remember you like me better as a rock?"

She shook her head, her gaze darting to his mouth before she looked everywhere in the cavern but at him. "We should look for a way out."

"We should," he agreed. "And we will." Just not yet.

He coaxed her a little closer, and slid his mouth over hers. She took her time parting her lips, as though she hadn't quite made up her mind to kiss him back. He didn't push, though, just savored the whisper of his mouth against hers until she locked her arms around his neck and took over.

Finding a way out of the catacombs suddenly seemed like an impossible task when he was lucky to remember his own name. Emma shifted in his lap and between one slow roll of her hips and the next, he was harder than the cavern walls. The next time she arched against him, he knew it was deliberate.

It also matched the teasing strokes of her tongue against his. Slow, lazy, teasing strokes that made him catch her hips and hold her still. Much more and they'd be finishing what they'd started in the woods. As much as he wanted that, he wanted her safe more, and they wouldn't be safe as long as they were lost in the catacombs.

Unable to stop instantly, he softened the kiss, drawing it out.

She finally drew back. "God, you're good at that."

He couldn't help but lean forward to catch her bottom lip one more time. "At distracting you?"

"There's distracting and there's making a girl completely lose her head."

It took him a minute to understand her meaning. "And that's bad?"

Sliding out of his lap, she stood and wandered toward the vines draping the cavern walls, muttering something that sounded a lot like, "Better my head than my heart."

She motioned to the pants she'd been using as a pillow, and he pulled them on while she wandered closer to one of the tunnels leading who knew where. “So, should we go with door number one?”

“Glamour?”

“Huh?”

“You said door. Do you see through some kind of glamour, like you did with that Fae?”

“No door. It’s just an expression. Catch up on your game shows and you’ll get it.”

“Game shows? Oh, like *Survivor.*” Although he still hadn’t figured out why the humans found it so challenging to live on an island when they spent most of their time sleeping or betraying one another.

She laughed. “Not quite.” She cocked her head, considering their options. “You’re the one with superior senses. What do you think?”

“That we need a map.” The tunnels all looked the same to him—vine-covered and twisting off around bends that made it impossible to guess what they’d be walking into.

“We’ll have to make do without unless there’s one stuffed in the pants you’re wearing.”

There was definitely something stuffed in his pants, and if he didn’t stop watching the strap from her bra slide off her shoulder, all the maps in this realm and the next wouldn’t stop him from finding his way up her shirt.

“How did you see through that Fae’s glamour?”

She stiffened next to him.

“I’ve never known a sorceress to be able to do that.”

“And have you known many sorceresses?” Her brows furrowed as she peeked down each tunnel, and he’d swear she sounded a little annoyed.

“Enough.”

"Apparently not or you'd know how I can do it. My mother is Fae." The expression on her face dared him to make something of it.

"I didn't think either race was particularly fond of each other."

She shrugged. "My mother must have remembered that after my sister and I were born."

"She left you?"

"My father has always favored the term abandoned." The moment she said father he could feel the tension radiate from her.

"You aren't on favorable terms with him."

"I'm his biggest disappointment." The casual answer couldn't fully mask the hurt in her voice. "What about your parents? Are you close to them?"

He nodded. "They went to stone three centuries ago." He hadn't been happy at the time, but knew his parents were five hundred years older than him, and eternity could be as dangerous to an immortal as fire or beheading.

"They chose to sleep at the same time? They must love each other very much."

He used to think maybe they'd loved one another too much. The last few weeks had given him a much better understanding of the bond between his parents.

"Is it because you're half Fae that you were able to enchant the mirror we used to cross over?"

"To be honest, I don't know. I haven't tried that since I was young."

"Why not?"

"I landed in a place so dark I couldn't see anything. I didn't know where I was, but I could hear creatures skulking around in the dark. They didn't come near me, but knowing they were there and that I couldn't see them was enough. I'm sure they were just as afraid of me as I was of them, but it's hard to be that objective when you're a frightened child."

"Who found you?"

"My mother. It was just before she left. It took two days, though, and by then I'd lost my voice from yelling. But that was a long time ago."

"For an immortal that can still feel like yesterday," he reminded her, echoing her words from earlier. "So why this time? You must have been afraid."

"I was more afraid of losing—" Her gaze darted away, but he could have sworn she'd been about to say "you".

He nodded to the tunnel on the left. "That one." Standing in front of it, he felt the same spark as when Emma used her magic, and he found the pull of it just as strong.

They walked in silence, the shadowy tunnel twisting along without any other tunnels branching off it.

"Why—"

She wheeled on him. "If we're about to play twenty questions, I get a turn. How did you catch those arrows at Leah's loft?"

"I have no idea."

"So that wasn't some gargoyle Guard training?"

He shook his head. "That's new." There had been barely enough time to wonder how he'd managed it. He'd felt stronger since Emma had broken the curse, more aware, but the cat was only concerned with tracking its mate, leaving him little time to dwell on it.

Emma glanced down at her palms. "I know what that's

like."

"Because you're used to being able to use your magic? Is that why you can no longer mask your tracings?"

"What do you mean?"

"The one at your throat."

She gave him that look, the one that questioned whether he should be locked up in an asylum. "I don't have one there."

"You do now. But it's...different. In between the ivy there are other symbols, like a Fae glyph. I've never seen anything like it." He crouched and drew the spiral in the dirt.

Her eyes widened. "How?" She glanced again at her palms as if she'd find something written there.

"You're the sorceress."

If she had an explanation for it, she didn't volunteer anything, and he was increasingly distracted by the magic that pulsed beneath his skin, like it was alive. They followed the tunnel until it branched to three. He chose the middle one without opposition from Emma.

"Something isn't right," he said a short while later. "We've hit a dead end."

"Of course we have." Emma sank to the ground. "It would have been too much to ask to find a way out without spending a decade or two wandering around." She let out a breath and closed her eyes.

Cian sat next to her, and the blossoms on the vines brightened.

"Whoa." The glowing light returned to its usual glow, though some blossoms remained bright pink and yellow. "Do you think that was normal?"

"You're asking the man who spent five hours trying to figure out how a remote control worked?" He wouldn't mention the time he contemplated the workings of an electric razor.

She smiled. “That’s different. This is Avalon. It’s home.” She leaned into him, and he was afraid to move in case it scared her off.

“It stopped being home the moment Morgana took Camelot.” And if Arthur’s half-sister got her hands on the daggers and Excalibur, all of Avalon would be at her mercy.

“It must have been hard for you, losing something you had helped to build.”

“Everyone lost something that day. I was just one among many.”

She held his gaze. “That doesn’t make your pain any less important.”

He might have dismissed another’s sympathy, eager to change the subject, but with Emma it felt as though she truly understood. Like she wasn’t just guessing how he’d felt when they’d lost Arthur and then Camelot, but felt the loss that shadowed his heart as if it were her own.

Catching her chin in his palm, he drew her close, softly covering her mouth with his. There was no explosion of need or urge to mark her, though both hovered just beneath the surface. He kissed her because he wanted to, not because he needed to, and the exquisite pleasure threatened to turn his whole world upside down.

Emma couldn’t breathe, and as much as she wanted the kiss to last, wanted to feel the heat of his mouth against hers for a lifetime, she was pretty damn sure it was killing her. The way he held her, like something treasured, like she was so much more than something he craved, the harder she fought to keep from giving him any more of her heart.

And she was going to lose. Maybe she already had.

Only when she whimpered against his lips did he pull back. His forehead touched hers, and they stayed that way until her pulse began to slow.

"Do you miss your jacket?"

"What, you don't think women in ripped, bloody tank tops are hot?"

"I don't wish to see any more of you covered up than necessary." His smile was wicked to the core. "Maybe not even then."

She bumped him with her shoulder.

"But do you miss it? You seemed awfully fond of it."

"When I'm wearing my jacket, people can't make snap judgments about me based on my tracings."

"Ah. You'd rather they underestimate your strength."

The predator in him would appreciate that, she supposed, and she was sure that Elena shared a similar mentality. "I'd rather they see me and not the magic." She leaned back against the wall. It was crazy to think that Cian of all people would get it.

He frowned. "I used to get into trouble. Often. I'd even foolishly pick fights so others would know I was just as tough as my older brothers. I needed people to respect me because of what I could do, what *I* stood for, not Cale and Tristan."

Maybe the gargoyle understood after all.

"How old were you when you joined the Guard?"

"Old enough to wield a sword but still too young to know I didn't always need it."

She cocked her head. "You can shape-shift into a vicious predator and you used a sword?"

"When the occasion called for it. But it's the same thing. If any of us learned to rely solely on a weapon or our animal halves, we wouldn't achieve the peace Camelot stood for."

"I wish I could have seen it."

"You've never walked the wall? Never seen Avalon stretch across the horizon at sunset, or when the moon is full and the sky so clear you can see every star in the heavens?"

"Not all of us are as old as you."

"Exactly how old are you?"

With a wink she stood and started back the way they'd come. "Guess we try another tunnel."

"How old?" he pressed, falling into step beside her.

"Old enough to know a woman should never answer that question."

He scoffed, then slanted a look at her abdomen. "Did that sound just come from your stomach?"

Her stomach had been rumbling since she'd woken up. "I happen to be starving." And had been doing a pretty good job of ignoring that fact until he brought it up. Neither of them would die from starvation, but that didn't mean they wouldn't be severely weakened by it.

Her feet felt blistered and her knees ached before they hit another dead end. "We're not getting anywhere."

Cian looked as frustrated as she felt as they backtracked to try another tunnel. "Some kind of water source must be feeding the vines, and where there's water, there's food. We're not giving up."

"I know. I'm just worried about my sister."

"If she's anything like you, she's probably giving them hell."

Undoubtedly. "We're not that much alike, actually. She's much bolder and braver than I am."

"I find that hard to believe."

She laughed. "If you hear her tell it, I used to be the bossy one, but I think she just tells me that so I wouldn't dwell on..." She trailed off, following Cian's gaze, forgetting what she'd been about to say.

"I don't remember that, do you?" He pointed to a vine that snaked across the top of a tunnel. A large red blossom with a buttery-yellow center hung in the middle.

"No." The longer she studied the crimson petals the more it intrigued her, drawing her closer.

"This way." He laced his fingers through hers, leading the way down a tunnel that grew increasingly narrow and sloped downward. Cian tipped his head. "I think I hear water."

Just hearing the word made her throat squeeze as though to wring even the slightest moisture from it. The tunnel twisted more sharply, the path growing steeper. The vines that grew along the wall pulsed with color.

That was either a good thing or they were in a whole world of trouble. She tightened her hold on Cian.

"Watch your st—"

Cian dropped in front of her, the ground giving way beneath him, and the fierce grip he had on her hand dragged her right along with him. The tunnel blurred past in bursts of green, pink and yellow, then the ground disappeared beneath them altogether.

Shit.

She lost her grip on Cian as they dropped straight down. Air whipped across her face and they plunged into the lake below, momentum pushing her down. The water closed over her head, and she kicked hard to reach the surface.

"Emma!" Cian grabbed her around the waist a moment

before she realized her feet just skimmed the sandy bottom. "Are you all right?"

She dropped her head against his shoulder. "Don't worry. I don't melt in water, Dorothy."

"Am I supposed to know what that means?"

She smiled, her lips parting to share the reference, but it slipped away before she could grasp it. Something about Oz?

He turned them toward the shore.

Shivering, she got as close to him as she could. "The water is freezing." Who would have believed an arctic glacier fed the catacombs? She paused. Is that where they were? The catacombs?

"I can see that."

She followed his gaze to where her nipples jutted against her shirt.

He smoothed her hair away from her face and that intense look in his eyes did crazy things to her stomach. He bent his head and she put a finger to his lips.

"As much as I'd love to be worked over by your very talented mouth, I'm a little distracted by the thought of what creatures might call this lake home."

Glancing around, he frowned. "Where are we?"

"We're..." She paused. "I..." Shook her head, wishing the answer would shake loose. She was sure she knew it. Wasn't she? "How did we get here?"

He shrugged, rubbing his cheek against hers. "Does it matter?"

"Yes?" Her eyes drifted shut as his lips grazed hers. "I can't remember." The harder she tried to bring the memories into focus, the faster they seemed to slip away from her.

Taking a step away from him, hoping the distance would

offer some clarity, she waded toward shore. On the grass, she sat and pulled off her boots, dumping out the water before wringing out her hair.

"Don't go yet."

She lifted her head, taken aback by the picture he made standing waist deep in the lake, drops of water sliding down his bare chest. The blossoms blanketing the ceiling at least a couple hundred feet above reflected on the lake's surface, like something out of a dream.

Her breath lodged in her throat as she watched him emerge and offer a hand.

"Come."

"Where are we going?"

He only offered a secretive smile and didn't wait for her agreement before pulling her to her feet. She went to grab her boots, but he swept her up, over his shoulder. Her surprised squeal carried across the lake, but the view of his ass in pants plastered to his skin was more than worth the blood rushing to her head.

He set her down as quickly as he'd picked her up, and she latched onto him until the dizziness passed.

"No more carrying me around without some advance warning."

Not looking the least bit apologetic, he tugged her across the soft grass and into the trees.

"Wow." She stared at the massive tree trunks that stretched toward the vine-covered ceiling. More vines twined around the branches, as if they were part of the tree, the flowers pulsing with vibrant colors that grew brighter at regular intervals.

Something brushed against her. Something furry. She

stumbled back, landing on her ass. The black cat curled around her, his tail snapping the ends of her hair. Unafraid, she swatted it away, watching the cat leap over a fallen log before glancing back at her, waiting.

Laughing, she got to her feet, looking once more over her shoulder at the lake that was already half concealed by a copse of trees. She could barely keep up, the cat easily staying ahead of her and occasionally doubling back and sneaking up behind her. Each time she'd get close, he'd disappear around a tree.

He was playing with her. She grinned and changed course the next time he vanished from view, moving in the opposite direction of the cat.

Two strong arms snared her around the waist, dragging her back against a warm, solid chest. He nuzzled her neck. "Did you think to trick me, mate?"

Mate? Yes, his. Always his.

"Crossed my mind."

"It's not wise to tease me."

She turned in his arms. "Plan to get even?"

He ran his fingers down her stomach. "I have so much more in mind than revenge." He unsnapped her pants. "Much, much more."

And then he was beneath her panties, his fingers parting her folds.

She moaned against his mouth. "Tell me."

He nipped her lip. "First I will fill you with my fingers, sinking into your softness until I make you good and wet for me." He circled her opening. "And then I'll kiss you. Here," he growled against her ear as his fingers circled her clit. "You'll feel my tongue sliding up your sex before I lick the most sensitive part of you."

Hot and breathless from the carnal imagery, she clung to him. “And then what?”

“You’ll feel such pleasure, you’ll move your hips and use your hands to pull me harder against you.” He moved his mouth, speaking low in her other ear. “You’ll be so close to release, you’ll be begging me to let you come.”

She was so close now, imagining his mouth tasting her long and deep. “Yes.”

“And right when you’re ready to find your release, your whole body on fire for it…I’ll stop,” he murmured.

“Yes…no.” She opened her eyes. “You can’t stop.”

“I can’t?” The wicked glimmer in his eyes said he could do whatever naughty, dirty things he wanted, and that she’d love every second of it.

She shook her head, knowing it wouldn’t come to that, even if she did beg. “No.”

He dragged her shirt over her head. “And why is that?” He palmed her breast, his thumb dragging across her nipple.

She whimpered. “You won’t be able to stop. You’ll need to have me.” Have all of her.

His sexy grin widened as if he understood her perfectly. “Don’t I have you now?”

Catching his jaw in her palm, she nodded. “Until the day I die.”

Chapter Ten

Cian took possession of her mouth, the way she had his heart, body and immortal soul. Everything in his mind was a blur, except her. Her he knew, recognized when everything around them felt foreign and unfamiliar.

His mate clung to him, her nails scoring his shoulders as she rose up to meet each wild kiss, taking parts of him he had never imagined sharing with anyone. And still it wasn't enough.

As if she caught a glimpse of his thoughts and was just as shaken, she broke away from his mouth, breathing hard. He didn't stop her when she slowly backed away from him, but he watched her every move. This he knew as well, certain they'd played this game before, and the moment he took a step toward her, he could tell by the expression on her face that she felt it too.

"You like chasing me."

He shook his head. "No. I like catching you." And he did, moving so fast there was no opportunity for her to escape him. He needn't have bothered since she waited for him, bracing herself as he swept her up and lowered her to the ground.

Easing between her legs, he flexed his hips and rubbed against her.

She arched beneath him, her breasts rising up, and he bent to trap one dark tip between his lips. She cried out, and he flicked his tongue across her nipple before moving on to the other.

Pinning her wrists to the ground, he hovered over her. She was so smart and beautiful and not afraid to stand up to him. He couldn't remember how he knew those things, but he felt them with every fiber of his being. She was perfect, and he was going to make her his.

He scraped his teeth along the edge of her jaw, then moved down her neck. "I need you. Now." He tugged her pants all the way down before catching her hip and easing her open for him. "I need to be inside you. Need to make you mine."

"I already am. Yours."

Growling in triumph, he sank inside her in one hard thrust. They both cried out, and he withdrew, holding her gaze as he filled her again. She squeezed her thighs around him, trapping him deep. Her muscles clenched around him, and he ground his jaw to keep from exploding inside her.

He started to withdraw, the fierce need to plunge into her running hot through his veins, only to hesitate at the vulnerability he glimpsed in her eyes.

"Be careful," she murmured, and he knew without asking it wasn't her body she worried about.

"Always."

She trapped his face between her hands and dragged him down to meet her mouth. He slid his arms beneath her knees, getting as deep as he could. She wrapped her arms around his neck, keeping him close as he pumped his hips faster, lost to the carnal rhythm.

Her back bowed, her sex clenching him so tight the pleasure of her climax nearly killed him. Buried inside her, he reveled in the feel of her release, her body slowly softening beneath his—until he couldn't hold back any longer and pounded into her.

Tension, sweet and hot, raced across his skin. So incredible. So close. So...

Ecstasy knifed through him, and he bent his head, surrendering to the cat's instinct to mark her as his forever.

Warmth nestled against him, and Cian lifted his head to find his mate curled around him. He closed his eyes, torn between falling back asleep and figuring out if everything still worked after they'd exhausted each other.

Without the sun or a watch, he couldn't begin to guess how long they'd been asleep. Minutes? Hours?

One part of his body didn't seem to care either way, and his mate chose that moment to roll against him, pressing into his arousal. He groaned, the sound stirring the gorgeous female who raised her head to study him.

A seductive smile curved her lips. "Hi." She stretched, and when he groaned a second time, she caught on to his problem.

Before he could pin her beneath him, she curled her fingers around him, pumping slowly. He hissed out a breath, watched her slide down his body. She ran the flat of her tongue up his cock from base to tip.

He dropped his head back to the ground, drugged by the sensation of her mouth taking him deep. After only a few teasing pulls, he raised his head to watch her again. Gods, she was incredible.

Her hair fell over her shoulder, revealing his mark at the curve where her shoulder met her neck, and his animal half roared in satisfaction. She was truly his.

And then all he could do was dig his fingers into the

ground, sliding a little faster between her lips. Her fingers curled around the base of his cock again, matching the feverish rhythm of her mouth.

Sweet Avalon.

Straining toward release, he begged her not to stop. She didn't, and moments later he shouted in pleasure.

Smiling, she threw her leg over his hip, straddling him as he tried to remember how to breathe. "Morning. Or maybe it's afternoon." She looked around them, her gaze suddenly unfocused. "Cian?"

He knew she was trying to remember something, but he quickly gave up trying to figure out what it might be when she shifted and the head of his cock grazed her sex. Soon he would have her again, and he had every intention of keeping her right where she was, so he could watch her ride him.

From the corner of his eye he saw something move, and he rolled to shield his mate beneath him.

"I come only to offer assistance."

A petite woman with long black hair pulled back in a braid stepped between the trees. Fae, and an old one at that despite her young appearance. Only the most ancient of the race had ears that were slightly pointed.

"I believe you two are lost."

His mate looked up at him. "Are we?"

No. At least he didn't think so. All he knew for certain was the sooner the Fae carried on about her business, the sooner he could be alone with the female drawing a teasing line down his abdomen.

The Fae wandered closer, cocking her head. "You two didn't take a swim in the lake by chance, did you?"

He thought it over, distracted when his mate squirmed

beneath him. "I don't believe there was a lot of swimming involved."

"Perfect," the Fae muttered. "And of all the places in Avalon, you would have to end up here."

Something about the Fae struck him as familiar. "Do I know you?"

"We've never been introduced before, no."

It wasn't really an answer, but he didn't care, not when his mate's leg brushed against his.

The Fae nodded in the direction she'd come from. "Best to get far away from the lake before you're tempted to take another dip."

Had that been what he'd been trying to remember earlier? That they needed to take a swim?

"The longer you're dried off," the Fae continued, "the sooner your memories will return." She turned, then stopped. "Maybe you didn't understand me?" She crossed her arms. "We're leaving. Now."

"Wait. I know you." His mate—Emma?—sat up, crossing her arms over her breasts. "I saw you…somewhere."

The Fae's eyes widened. "You marked her?" For a moment he thought she might faint. "I'll worry about fixing that later."

He growled low in his throat.

She rolled her eyes and glanced at Emma. "And that does something for you, really? I've never understood the attraction to gargoyles myself. I prefer my men more...submissive." She grinned, adjusting the bow strapped to her back. "I really meant it when I said it was time to leave. The lake's guardian tends to visit every few hours, and you don't want to tangle with him. He's six feet plus of mean dragon. The Forgotten," she added.

"Why are you helping us?"

She motioned to Emma. "I'm helping her. You just get to tag along."

Wary, he hesitated to let his mate go anywhere with an unfamiliar Fae. "Help us how?"

"By showing you how to get out of here."

Emma glanced at him. "We need to go. I just can't remember where."

"It'll come back to you." The Fae motioned to a pair of boots and clothing he had stripped off Emma earlier. "I'm fairly certain you're going to want to get dressed." She stared at the ground, then sighed. "You cats and your need to be naked."

A pair of pants materialized next to him.

"Better get a move on. There are others in the catacombs and you'll want to stay ahead of them."

Dragging his gaze away from Emma, who quickly pulled her clothes on, Cian yanked on the pants the Fae provided. "What others?"

"Less talking. More walking."

"If someone wants Emma..." He trailed off, something tugging at his memory.

"They'll have to go through you first. Got it." She glanced at Emma. "He is less chatty when he's doing his feline impression, right?"

He reached out and caught Emma's hand before the Fae got it into her head to try anything.

"Relax, puss, she's safe with me." Her bored expression said, *you, on the other hand...*

"My sister." Emma blurted. "I need to find my sister." Relieved, she smiled at Cian, and he felt a little dazed by the full intensity of it.

When they reached the edge of the woods, he stopped,

wondering if he and Emma were better off returning the way they'd come.

The Fae nudged Emma. "Take the next tunnel you come to, then the one on the left. Follow it until the vines start to thin and the blossoms are blue. Take the next right tunnel you come to. Stay in that one all the way out. Even when it looks like the tunnel ends, stay on it."

"Thank you..."

"Amelina." She stared at Emma a long moment, then held out a charm. "You can use this to summon me, but seeing as it's a one-shot deal, I'd save it for an emergency."

Emma tucked the charm in her pocket, frowning at the Fae.

"What if—" He stopped. Amelina had vanished, and he was left staring after Emma, who'd started ahead.

When he caught up to her, she wouldn't meet his eyes, and panic crept through him. She glanced back the way they'd come, and he stopped her.

"You're remembering, aren't you?"

"Some. You will too." She carefully touched his mark, her skin still healing.

"We don't have to leave." If leaving meant losing her smile, he'd stay and fight whatever monster came their way.

She turned on her heel, following the Fae's directions. "We can't. Even if we could, you wouldn't want to."

He picked up his pace, intent on catching up with her. "What is that supposed to mean?"

"It means to forget it."

"Forget what?" He caught her arm, jerking her to a stop.

"This. Everything." The sadness she tried to mask cut into him.

Running his fingers across his mark, he shook his head. "Neither of us will forget that." He flinched as the words left his mouth, as if suddenly uncomfortable in his own mind, and then everything came rushing back.

His hand dropped away from her, but not his gaze. He was too busy staring at his mark as if seeing it for the first time.

Fuck.

"Welcome back." She shot him a sideways glance and then started into the tunnel.

He almost didn't follow. He'd made it official, claimed her as his mate, something no magic could ever take back.

Losing sight of her, he sprinted to catch up. His muscles, like his brain, felt weighed down, but he didn't say anything when he caught up with her. Couldn't.

"You're glaring at me."

"No." He was just trying to figure out what the hell he was supposed to do now. Permanently bonding with her hadn't been part of his plan at all.

She snorted. "I can practically feel the daggers digging into my skin."

Would he ever understand her? "I'm not even armed." And if he was, there was a good chance he might have hunted down the Fae who was somehow responsible for his present situation.

"Well, you're looking at me like you're stuck with me forever."

He didn't say anything.

She stopped and faced him. "What?"

"I marked you."

"So things got a little out of hand. I'll get over it."

A little out of hand? "Maybe you will, but I won't. I marked you. Claimed you as my mate."

The blank look on her face finally gave way to understanding. Her lips parted, but it took another few moments for her to respond. "But what happened between us... We were...you and I..."

"Were acting on instinct." He didn't mean for it to sound so harsh, but she flinched anyway. Damn it.

She turned away from him. "Blue flowers."

He followed her gaze as they passed another tunnel branching off from the opposite side. He paused, backtracked. The seductive pulse of magic licked up his spine.

"Where are you going?"

A hundred times more potent than before, he couldn't ignore the pull of it any more than he had been able to ignore his attraction to Emma. "This way."

She sidestepped to block him. "That's not the way out. Look, I get that you're mad, but if we don't follow Amelina's directions, we're going to end up lost. Again."

Not lost. Found. "We need to go this way."

"Why?"

He had no idea, but admitting that would doubtfully earn her cooperation. "You need to trust me, Emma." He almost missed the narrow passageway that blended right into the vines. "It's in here."

Her grip on his arm stopped him from going any farther. "What is?"

He frowned, searching the darkness within. "Something we need."

"There aren't any vines in there." She eyed the walls skeptically. "I wish I could say I had been exaggerating earlier when I mentioned my issue with the dark, but I wasn't."

"You'll be fine, but if you're too scared, you can wait out here." Leaving her alone wasn't truly an option, but neither was ignoring whatever called to him.

Emma's shoulders snapped back, and she preceded him into the tunnel, reaching back at the last second for his hand.

His eyes quickly adjusted to the dark, his gaze drawn toward something twenty feet in that threw off its own glow. More blossoms?

"Whoa."

He paused next to Emma, staring at the weapon lodged in the tunnel wall. The silver hilt of the dagger pulsed brighter with every step he took toward it.

"Is that one of Constantine's?"

"I think so." He reached a hand out, but she stopped him inches from touching it.

"Maybe you shouldn't. Maybe it's some kind of catacombs booby trap and if you touch it spikes come out of the walls before they close in on us, or the ceiling starts to lower."

"It's not a trap." Without waiting, he pulled it from the wall, much the same way he imagined Arthur had once drawn Excalibur from the stone. "Incredible." The glow of the dagger was bright enough to hurt his eyes. He turned back the way they'd come, anxious to examine it in better lighting.

The ground underneath his feet shook, slamming him into the wall. Rocks rained down on them.

"Cian!"

Above them, the ceiling caved in, and he pitched forward, pushed from behind. He whipped around as the passageway collapsed behind him, sealing Emma inside.

Emma staggered back, the earth shaking so hard beneath

her feet she went down hard. Her head struck the cavern wall, and nausea gripped her stomach and wrenched hard.

Fighting the urge to empty her stomach, she glanced at the light slipping away with the slide of rocks and earth until the tunnel sucked up every last bit of it, plunging her into darkness. In a heartbeat she was a child again, terror thick in her throat as the dark came alive around her.

"No!" Her heart slammed against her ribs, and she sprang forward, clawing at the barrier.

"Emma!" Muffled by the earth separating them, she could barely hear him.

The stranglehold fear had on her lungs eased up just a bit. She wasn't a child anymore, wasn't alone. Vibrations carried across the barrier, and relief made it a little easier not to give into the panic tearing through her bloodstream. He was trying to dig her out.

"Hang on."

"Hurry!"

She must have sounded worse than she thought, because he quickly came back with, "Talk to me, Em."

"About what?"

"Who taught you to count cards?"

"Leah."

"The one who painted the mural?"

"Yeah. She's probably half out of her mind with worry by now. Not that she'd ever admit it." Leah was far too good at masking her emotions. Right now Emma wouldn't mind possessing a little more of that particular gift.

Light speared through the darkness, and hope flared in her chest. She scrambled up, pulling rocks out of the way until she caught a glimpse of his face.

"Just a little longer, okay?"

She nodded. "Okay."

He continued to dig, and more earth slid down to replace what he'd cleared away. The light was instantly extinguished, and she coughed from the dust released into the air.

"How long have you known her? What's she like?" She heard him start again, but refrained from trying to dig on this side, afraid she'd cause it to cave in again.

"Twenty years." Though sometimes it felt like forever. "She makes me laugh all the time and she loves Karaoke as much as she does gambling. And her favorite thing for breakfast is cold pizza." She shuddered. "I couldn't carry a tune to save my life and I prefer burgers to pizza any day of the week."

He groaned. "Let's not talk about burgers." She smiled at the longing in his voice.

"Move back!" He barely got the warning out before more of the ceiling started to come down.

Again, she heard him digging, but he didn't get far before the earth above them trembled.

"You don't need me to save you, Emma."

"And who will? The catacombs fairy?" He didn't laugh at her joke, which she took as a very bad sign.

"Every time I try to dig, it collapses. You have to do this."

"I'm not strong enough." She hadn't been strong enough as a child either, had needed her mother to find her.

"Yes, you are."

The conviction in his voice, a warrior that wouldn't let anyone admit defeat, almost made her grin. "You don't understand. My magic—"

"Is more than enough." He shoved more earth and rocks out of the way, and she blinked at the light that cut through the darkness “Here.”

It took her a second to recognize the feel of the dagger as she withdrew it from the small opening, then memories assailed her. She staggered under the overwhelming flashes as she felt the heat from the flames Constantine used to forge the weapon, her heart breaking at the knight’s regret for failing his king. Then the brush of powerful magic as the Lady of the Lake enchanted the dagger...

“Emma? Emma!”

She finally got her voice working, the memories fading as she concentrated on the sound of Cian’s voice. “I’m okay.”

“What happened? You weren’t answering me.”

“I think I forgot to mention that I can relive the memories tied to an object when I touch it.”

“Interesting trick.”

Not interesting enough to get herself out of the tunnel. “Cian, I can’t use this. There’s no way to predict what will happen.”

“You’ll be fine.”

His confidence in her, while insanely misplaced, nevertheless touched her. He almost made her feel like she could actually do it. “And what about you?”

“I’ll get out of the way.”

She shook her head. There had to be another option, one that didn’t involve using a powerful weapon to channel her hit-or-miss magic. “Cian—”

“Do it, Em.” That trademark arrogance was back in full force.

“Go back down the tunnel. You need to be clear just in case.” The other side of Avalon probably wasn’t even far enough away. This was Elena’s thing, not hers.

She closed her eyes, tightening her grip on the weapon. The power of the dagger crackled across her skin. It would be crazy to try something she'd never attempted. Better to use it to strengthen something she'd done before.

Holding the dagger in her left hand, she pulled energy into her right palm, let it burn hotter and hotter—and threw it at the rock barrier.

The purple flames dispersed on impact, the force of the blast knocking her backward. Not waiting to see if it would trigger another cave in, she scrambled to her feet and lunged through the opening.

She ran straight into another barricade, pushing it over as she toppled forward. Breathless, she raised her head and found herself looking down at Cian.

Her mouth fell open. "You didn't go farther down the tunnel?"

"I stood to the side."

"Are you out of your mind?" She didn't even know why she asked when he clearly was. "I could have blown you sky high."

Cian shrugged as though being reduced to kitty pulp wasn't a big deal. "I trusted you."

"You stupid, arrogant—"

He caught the back of her head and crushed her mouth to his. Only when her anger retreated and she softened against him did he loosen his hold on her.

"I trusted you," he said again, but with him continuing to sweep his mouth across hers, she could only come up with one response.

"Why?"

"Because you use your brain and not magic to win at cards. Because you put other people's needs ahead of your own, helping strangers on crutches and listening to your friend's problems, even when it's not always convenient for you. Because you're loyal and protective of your human friend and the sister you would do anything to save."

"And you thought all those reasons were good enough to trust me with something as powerful as the dagger?" The one she'd nearly unmanned him with, but if he noticed how close the blade had come to his groin when they'd collided, he didn't let on.

Wait. Something he'd said tugged at her memory. "Something you said about strangers on crutches—"

He pressed his finger to her lips. "Someone is coming." He pulled her to her feet.

She glanced down at the dagger, feeling nothing from the weapon. "Something's wrong with it."

Cian took it and tossed it into the narrow opening, and she knew it was better to hide it until they knew what they were facing. Too many people coveted the weapon to risk revealing its presence to just anyone.

He pulled her behind him just as four men came in to view. She recognized Urien immediately, his eyes—one green, one white—as creepy as ever.

How could they have tracked her through the catacombs? No one knew where they were... An oracle. Cian's family had used one to track her, even deep in Korrigan territory.

Two of the men parted and Elena was jerked to the front of the group by a chain fastened to very familiar restraints.

Shit.

Urien twirled the end of the chain. "Nice, huh? I really do appreciate you leaving these in a bag at your pet human's place. They've come in pretty handy."

Ignoring him, Emma focused on her sister. “You okay?”

Elena cocked her head, her gaze darting from Emma’s throat to Cian. “And here I was about to ask you the same thing.” A sly grin curved her lips. “I’m thinking you got the better end of the deal this time, Em. Except for Gareth.”

At the mention of the sorcerer’s name, Cian growled. She touched his shoulder, needing to soothe the cat she glimpsed in his eyes.

Urien pointed his sword at Elena’s back, a reminder of who had the advantage.

Elena glanced over her shoulder. “Is that it? So the saying is true. Little sword, little package.”

“I don’t need much of a reason to take your head,” Urien snapped.

“Why don’t you take these cuffs off and we’ll see if your balls are really made of brass or just pussy willows?”

He dug the tip of the sword into her nape, and Elena hissed.

“I’m surprised Gareth trusted you to bring me in.”

Urien’s attention predictably shifted to Emma. “You give yourself too much credit, love.” He cocked his head. “So this is the gargoyle who caught two arrows mid-air? Intriguing.”

“He has nothing to do with any of this.”

“Is that so?”

She nodded. “Wrong time and place.”

Urien gestured to the fierce grip Cian had on her. “I get the impression your pet thinks otherwise.” He tsked. “I had thought you of all people had higher standards, Emma.”

“Happy to have disappointed you.”

He jerked his head at the guy closest to Emma. “Bring her.”

Her. Not them. However, her momentary relief that Cian was going to be left out of it evaporated the second Elena stepped forward.

"You really don't want to leave him behind."

Emma braced herself, recognizing her sister's tone, positive she wasn't going to like whatever came next.

"The gargoyle was cursed by one of Constantine's daggers."

Chapter Eleven

Cian glanced back and forth between the two women glowering at each other from opposite sides of their cell.

Twins. Identical twins. Being trapped with two beautiful women might be a fantasy come true for some men, but for Cian, it just made his head hurt.

Twins.

It had only taken one look at Elena's numerous tracings to figure out which of them had actually cursed him. What he hadn't been able to figure out was why Emma hadn't told him the truth, and where all of that left him—aside from trapped in a sorcerer's dungeon.

Emma pivoted from the iron door that had slammed shut only moments ago. "Why in the hell did you tell them about Cian being cursed?"

Elena shrugged. "Seemed like a good idea at the time."

"Really? The way you thought castrating a dragon was a good idea?"

If Cian didn't know better, he'd swear Emma was about to unleash her animal half.

"He had it coming, and besides, it was just temporary." Elena rolled her eyes, and he got the impression this wasn't the first time they'd had this kind of conversation.

"Or the time you cast an enchantment spell and made a wraith fall in love with one of Morgana's trolls?"

"You have to admit, they were a damn cute couple." She glanced at Cian. "In that so-ugly-it's-cute kind of way."

Emma wasn't amused, her cheeks flushed with an angry color he'd been on the receiving end of more than once. "And what about this time?"

"I would have kept my mouth shut if I'd known you were in love with the gargoyle."

"I..." Emma seemed to remember he was in the room. She'd been preoccupied with her sister ever since they'd followed Urien's markings out of the catacombs and were transported—by dragon no less—to the sorcerer's castle and locked up. "It would just be really nice if you could behave for a decade or two."

"And how much fun would you have then?"

Emma's eyes nearly popped right out of here head. "Fun? Seriously?"

Elena crossed her arms. "So you two haven't had any fun? 'Cause I'm guessing there must have been at least a little fun going down for that to happen." She pointed at the nearly healed mark he'd put on Emma.

"It's not what you think."

Elena snorted. "What? You tripped and fell on his teeth?"

He fought a grin before remembering that Emma's twin was right at the top of his list of least favorite people.

"It's not like that."

"So that's not a mate's mark on your shoulder?"

"It's complicated."

When Elena glanced at him, he only shrugged, staying out of it for now. He knew from experience that it was better to let siblings get it out of their system. Half the time Cale had come away more scratched up than he or Briana when he broke up one of their arguments.

She turned back to Emma. "And I suppose that's my fault too?"

"As a matter of fact, yes."

Looking annoyed, Elena stalked toward his mate. "Is there anything you don't blame me for?"

"Is there something here that isn't your fault?"

Elena threw her hands up in the air. "God, maybe you can talk some sense into her."

Taking that as his cue, he straightened from the wall he'd been leaning against since the two had started with each other.

"Why did you do it?" He'd been wondering for weeks, had given up on getting an answer out of Emma. At least now he understood why she had never offered an explanation.

Emma, who'd paced in his direction a moment ago, stopped in her tracks. He hadn't let on that he'd figured out which twin was really to blame for his imprisonment. He could tell by the expression on Elena's face when she turned toward him that she'd been anticipating the question for a while.

"I overestimated my control."

"So why not undo it then?" Emma asked.

"I was a little freaked out at the time, and his brother nearly took a chunk out of my hide, so I bailed."

"Leaving him like that permanently."

"Not intentionally." Elena sighed. "Come on, Em. You know I'm not that heartless. Most of the time," she tacked on at the end.

For the first time he saw regret flash in Elena's eyes. "I did try to undo it and nothing worked. So I went with a counter spell, but I just assumed it never took since I thought he was still doing his masonry impression until a few days ago."

She frowned and glanced again at the mark on Emma. "Ah." Satisfaction gleamed in her eyes, and he realized her counter spell must have been tied to his mate.

If Elena had tried to make it so that his mate could break the spell with her proximity, then when Emma ended up on the roof with him...

He was such as ass. All this time he'd believed their bond was related to some kind of enchantment spell, had fought his instincts, and the cat had been right all along.

"Ah?" Emma snapped. "That's all you have to say?"

"So I should apologize for getting you two together?"

This time Emma's voice actually cracked with anger. "You want credit for making him think I'm his mate, all thanks to your enchantment spell?"

Elena shook her head. "Enchantment spell?"

Cian whirled on Emma before her sister said anything more. He knew the lengths his mate went for the people she cared about. She'd let herself be held prisoner for days to protect her sister. If she knew his feelings for her were genuine, she'd feel even more responsible for him. She spent enough time worrying about other people. He refused to burden her with his real feelings while they were locked up.

"When were you planning on telling me you weren't the one who trapped me in stone?"

She blinked. "I did try to tell you a couple times."

He crossed his arms.

She blew out a breath. "Look, I didn't think you'd be all that quick to help me find Elena if you knew the truth."

"You would have been right." He was still angry with her

twin, but not as much as he was himself. At the same time he knew if not for the curse, if not for his family tracking the wrong sorceress, it might have been centuries before their paths crossed.

Seeming to read his mind as easily as her sister, Elena gave him a smug look. "I like red. Rubies, designer clothes, sports cars. Just something to keep in mind when you're shopping for an appropriate thank you gift."

"Unbelievable," Emma muttered.

"I don't know about you guys, but I am starving." Elena wandered over to the door. "Who does a girl have to curse around her to get some food?"

When Emma took a step toward her twin, Cian snagged her wrist, coaxing her in the opposite direction. Fully embracing their bond and accepting that Emma was truly his, left him calmer than he'd felt in weeks. Now that both man and cat were at peace with each other, he could focus entirely on getting his mate as far from the sorcerer as he could.

Emma dropped onto the bench beneath the cell's only window, the bars over it fortified by Fae magic. She stared at their joined hands and carefully slid hers free. "I'm sorry I didn't tell you everything. If I had, you might not have followed me out of the casino that day."

"I would have followed you through the catacombs."

"We already did that."

"We did, didn't we?" He lifted her hand to his face, indulging in the warmth of her palm on his skin. "Then you might as well give up trying to get rid of me."

"Don't do that."

Hearing the pain in her voice, he frowned. "What?"

"Don't make me fall even harder for you."

"Even if I vow to catch you?"

She shook her head, but before she could voice another objection, he touched his forehead to hers. He didn't take it any further than that at first, marveling over her quick intake of breath and the way her fingers trembled.

"Cian," she whispered, and her voice caught him hard in the chest.

Opening his mouth over hers, his plans to distract her were lost the second she boldly stroked her tongue across his. Between one breath and the next, he couldn't remember what he'd even wanted to distract her from in the first place. He knew only Emma's addictive taste, the feel of her lips and the certainty that enchantment or not, she had him completely under her spell.

Elena cleared her throat. "As much as I hate to break up your fun, our favorite Fae is coming down the hall, and he's not alone."

A moment later Urien opened the cell door, and Cian got his first look at the sorcerer who coveted his mate. Gareth was a couple inches shorter than him, his hair dark and long, his expression calculating as he dismissed Elena by turning his back on her.

The sorcerer's hard green gaze bypassed Emma altogether, landing on the grip Cian had on her. There was only a whisper of warning before an invisible hand closed around his throat and pinned him against the wall.

"Stop!"

Cian reached out to prevent his mate from moving toward Gareth, but the grip around his throat tightened.

"You got what you wanted. I'm here. You have no need for them." If the scent of her fear didn't overwhelm him, he might have believed she was as calm as she appeared.

As if he'd grown bored already, Gareth released him, his attention focused on Emma. "Oh?"

"And my father won't tolerate you holding Elena prisoner."

"Permanently, no. But he knows she is my guest until the ceremony is complete."

"Lying son of a bitch," Elena snarled.

Gareth cocked his head, moved closer to Emma. "That's a very interesting tracing." Catching Cian's eye, the sorcerer drew his finger across her throat.

Cian betrayed no response—though he sure as hell wanted to—knowing it was exactly what Gareth wanted.

Sighing, the sorcerer let his arm drop back to his side. "I look forward to discovering what other surprises you have in store for me, Emma. As soon as you've scrubbed every trace of the cat off you."

"Let them go and I swear you'll have my full cooperation."

Gareth laughed, the sound making Cian ache to bury his fist in his face. "I'm afraid I need more time to find the best way to utilize the gargoyle's exposure to the dagger's magic, and when I do, I'll want him on hand."

"If you have him, you don't need Emma," Elena pointed out.

"My family is expecting an alliance between our houses today." He tipped his head toward Cian. "He's no more than an early wedding present which I'm very grateful to Emma for."

"Screw you."

"Oh, I intend to."

Snarling, Cian lunged for the bastard.

"Don't." Emma planted herself in front of him.

Gareth smirked. "Already she protects me, gargoyle."

Elena snorted. “Get over yourself. It’s him she’s protecting. He’d slash your throat out in a blink, but by then Urien would be on him.”

Not appearing to like hearing that, he motioned to Urien. “Take her to my rooms to prepare for the ceremony.”

“I’ll be fine,” Emma insisted when Cian refused to let her go. “You know I’ll be okay.”

Did he? The only thing he was dead certain of was how much he wanted to sink his claws into Gareth.

Elena stepped up next to him. “She can handle herself.” Admiration laced her words. “She’s gotten me out of worse situations than this.” She caught Emma’s hand and gave it a quick squeeze.

Urien laughed. “That would be something to see.”

Looking as confident as an oracle, Elena smiled. “Pull up a chair.”

“Enough.” Gareth headed for the door. “Come along, Emma.”

The moment Urien closed the door to Gareth’s room, Emma dug Amelina’s charm out of her pocket.

“Amelina of the Fae, I wish to make a bargain.”

“A bargain? I remember telling you to use the charm in case of emergency.”

Emma whipped around, quickly matching the Fae’s militant stance. “I see your leg has healed nicely.”

She didn’t appear surprised Emma had remembered her from the casino.

“Why were you there?”

"You didn't summon me just to ask that."

"That's not the only reason, no. Gareth, the sorcerer who's been after me, plans to kill Cian, the gargoyle I was with in the catacombs." There wasn't a doubt in Emma's mind Gareth would dispose of him the moment he stopped being useful, and she had no intention of letting that happen.

"And that's where the bargain comes in?"

Emma nodded. "There was a dagger in the catacombs."

The Fae sighed, sliding into a chair in front of the sprawling stone fireplace. The gesture instantly reminded her of Elena when she settled in to listen to Emma be *reasonable*. "And I suppose you want my help retrieving Constantine's dagger?"

Emma froze. "You already took it, didn't you? Is that why you were in the casino? You suspected Cian could somehow lead you to one?"

"My reasons for being in the casino had nothing to do with the gargoyle, until I saw the way he was looking at you."

Emma shook her head, unable to make sense of what Amelina was saying. "Why would you care how he was looking at me?"

The Fae gave her a sad smile. "Mine have always been one of the few glamours you could never see through, you know."

"Glamour?"

Before her eyes, the Fae's appearance morphed, aging her.

Holy Shit. "Leah? But you're...human," she settled on for lack of a better word. "Why didn't you tell us?" Tell them, show them, draw them a picture. Something.

The glamour faded once more. "It's complicated. I wanted to tell both you and Elena, but I'm not supposed to have contact with either of you for another century." Her voice was close, but a little higher than what Emma was used to.

"I don't understand." Not even a little bit. "You're Fae?" Maybe if she said it aloud a few times, her brain would process it.

"I am."

Behind them the door opened, and her father stepped inside. Even though Gareth had mentioned him, she had no idea he was here. Roan was nearly six hundred years old but still looked to be in his late twenties, his hair so much lighter than hers and Elena's, but he had the same gray eyes.

"I know you're mad at me," he began, then stopped when he saw she wasn't alone. His expression paled before his eyes narrowed. "What the hell are you doing here?"

"You two know each other?" Her father's appearance was surprising all on its own and now this...

Her father stepped up beside her, glaring at Leah. "You're not supposed to be here."

"And you're not supposed to be marrying her off to Gareth or anyone else for the sake of an alliance, but that's not stopping you."

"You lost the right to have a say when you left us."

Emma held up a hand. "What did you say?"

Her father frowned at her.

"She doesn't know," Leah said quietly. "Or she didn't until you opened your big mouth."

Dropping into the chair Leah had vacated, she glanced back and forth between them...between her parents?

She opened her mouth but nothing came out. Not a word. Not even a syllable. The ache in her chest that she'd been doing her best to ignore since Urien had learned of Cian's tie to the dagger, clamped down like a vise.

"Is she going to faint?"

"Of course not," Leah answered, then crouched next to her.

"Don't pretend you know anything about her," her father snapped.

"I know a hell of a lot more than you do." She searched Emma's eyes, lowering her voice. "Do you need a paper bag?"

She shook her head, digging her hands into her palms in an effort to hold off the emotional upheaval of the last couple days. The last few minutes guaranteed it would be a losing battle.

Leah was her mother. Leah, who was her best friend next to Elena, someone she got drunk with, laughed with, grew annoyed with, and all this time...

"This wasn't how I pictured you finding out."

"You shouldn't have come back." Her father glanced at Emma, and for the first time in decades, she saw genuine concern in his eyes.

Leah stood and whirled. "And you should have stopped Gareth from hunting our daughters like animals."

"Now they're *our* daughters? How convenient."

"You were the one who refused to let me see them."

Out of nowhere a memory slammed into Emma's mind. She'd woken up in her bed, a scream caught in her throat. Another nightmare, like the ones she'd been having for months after being lost in the catacombs.

Spotting the candle her father made sure never went out during the night, she realized she was safe in her bed, and had lain back, closing her eyes. She'd barely drifted off again when she heard voices outside her room. She'd slipped from her bed and crept into the hall to hear her father arguing with someone.

"Don't do this, Roan, I need to see them."

"No."

"You can't—"

"You made your choice." Her father had turned then, spotting Emma. "Leave now," he'd said over his shoulder, then strode toward his daughter, his big body preventing her from seeing who he had been talking to.

"Let's get you tucked back in bed, angel." He kissed her forehead, and she peeked over his shoulder, but the room behind him was empty.

Shaken by the memory, she glanced at Leah. "You came to see us."

"A handful of times," her father said, a whisper of disappointment beneath the anger.

"Only to be refused every single time."

Her father scoffed. "We both know you had the means to succeed if you really wanted to be there."

"I was trying not to hurt you any more than I had to. You know I had no choice, and you refused to come with me."

"A sorcerer in the Fae court?"

Fae court? Emma took a longer look at Leah. Only Fae royalty was part of the court.

"And it was no place for halfling daughters," he continued. "Even your mother realized that. It was only a matter of time before someone tried to use them as pawns against Titania."

Titania? Queen Titania?

"And how long was I gone before you made arrangements with Gareth's family for an alliance? A week? A month? Two? Power has always been all that mattered to you."

"After you walked away, it was all I had left."

"No." Emma stood. "You had me and Elena."

Surprise registered on his face, then his shoulders slipped

a little. "I..." He shook his head, and Emma felt like she was seeing her father as more than just cold and proud. She remembered blaming him when their mother left, accusing him of sending her away.

Now each time he glanced covertly at Leah, she could see he'd been just as devastated as she and Elena.

"You need to fix this," Leah told him.

His expression darkened. "Don't tell me what to do, Lee."

"Well someone needs to. Emma can't marry Gareth."

"He's still young and overzealous, but he's powerful, well connected. He can protect her. She might even come to care for him."

Leah took a step toward him, reaching a hand out to touch him. Her father eased back, a glimmer of something—fear?—in his eyes.

Her chin dropped. "Is that really what you want for her?"

"Following her heart isn't any more of a guarantee that she'll be happy." Old pain echoed in his voice.

"Tell that to the gargoyle she loves, the one who marked her." Leah pulled Emma's hair back, exposing the faint scar.

"*What?*"

If her father could have a heart attack, Emma was pretty sure she was seconds away from having to perform CPR.

"When the hell did that happen?"

The stern look on his face instantly transported Emma back to her childhood. "Yesterday."

"And the gargoyle still lives?" His gaze snapped to Leah's.

Emma rolled her eyes. The gods save her from men who chose the wrong moment to get overprotective. "Gareth has him locked up with Elena at the moment."

"If the gargoyle did that without your consent..." her father began.

"The way you made arrangements to marry me off without care for what I wanted?"

Her father paled. "I was..." He cleared his throat, tried again.

"I believe the word you're looking for is wrong."

He scowled at Leah, who shrugged in the same casual way Elena did. Holy crap, Elena was going to freak when she found out about Leah. About their mom.

"Gareth plans to use Cian, or the dagger magic that infused him somehow, and when he's done with him..." Emma swallowed, more resolved than ever to prevent him from hurting Cian.

"You do love him," Leah said softly.

Emma nodded. "He's insanely possessive and arrogant and stubborn. And I'm still crazy about him, even though I know when Elena breaks her enchantment spell, his feelings for me will fade."

Leah's brows crashed together. "Elena didn't do an enchantment spell."

"How do you know?"

"When your daughter uses one of Constantine's daggers to curse a gargoyle, you hear about that kind of thing."

Her father gave them both a blank look.

"Some people hear about those things," Leah corrected.

"She tried a counter spell, but it didn't work."

Leah smiled. "Not until you came along?"

"Right."

"Because she's his mate." Her father looked pleased that

he'd put it together without anyone having to explain anything.

Feeling the need to sit before she did faint, Emma dropped back into the chair. She really was Cian's mate?

"Emma—"

She held her hand up at her father, needing another minute to let it sink in, and also because she was a smidge annoyed that her father, who'd been in the dark about almost everything until a few minutes ago, had figured it out before her. Figured it out—

"He knows." She pushed to her feet. "Cian cut Elena off in the cell when I was asking her about it. The sneaky feline knows."

Her father looked grim. "Emma, Gareth will be here any moment. He said he would be right along when I passed him on my way to see you."

"He won't willingly release Cian."

"So we'll make him." Leah held something out to her. The dagger.

"Is that what I think it is?" Her father bumped into her getting a closer look.

"Try not to drool, Roan. Here." Leah pushed it into Emma's hand.

Like the last time in the tunnel, she didn't feel a damn thing. "I don't have the power to use it."

"Yes, you do."

"I tried in the tunnel. The first time was just a fluke."

Leah shook her head. "You just have to believe in yourself, baby."

She made it sound so easy, and it probably would be for her. "My magic is too unpredictable, when it works at all."

Leah scanned the room, leaving her side just long enough to grab a handheld mirror. “You see that?” She held the mirror up so Emma could see her new tracing. “The Fae glyphs are there because you’ve begun to tap into your Fae magic. It’s still new and unfamiliar, like when you were a child, but it’s there.”

She shook her head and tried giving the dagger back to Leah.

Her father stiffened next to her. “Maybe you shouldn’t have such high expectations of her, Lee.”

“And maybe yours aren’t high enough,” Leah challenged. She dismissed him with a scowl. “You know how Elena jokes that you used to be the wild one? That’s because it’s true. You were fearless with magic, but yours was always different, your strengths laid in your Fae heritage and when you tried crossing the veil and ended up in the catacombs, you began to fear it.”

Emma glanced down at her palm. “Why now? Why am I able to tap into it after all this time?”

Leah simply stared at her, waiting.

“Cian,” she whispered to herself a moment later.

“Being in love can be incredibly powerful, can make us feel invincible.”

“She’s right.”

Leah glanced up at him, grateful that her parents weren’t glowering at each other at the moment. Progress.

Her father cleared his voice, glanced at Leah. “You should go before Gareth arrives.”

“If you’re suggesting I can’t handle myself—”

So much for a truce. “I’m sure you two have things you need to say to each other, but it needs to wait.” Emma turned toward Leah—her mother. Thinking of her that way felt unfamiliar, but comforting.

"Elena needs you. The cuffs she's wearing null her magic. And she's more capable of wielding the dagger."

"I'll bet your gargoyle would disagree with that." Leah closed Emma's fingers tighter around the weapon. "This dagger has been used in the catacombs where Fae magic is its most pure. You have the advantage over Elena this time." With that Leah vanished, making arguing with her a waste of breath.

Alone she glanced at her father, who stared at the spot where Leah had stood. "Is your head spinning as fast as mine?"

He grinned, and memories of seeing him smile when she and Elena were younger squeezed her heart. "Faster."

"Tell me something, gargoyle."

Cian shuddered in anticipation of Elena's next question. According to the sorceress, she had a tendency to ramble when she was starving, and judging by the fact that she'd barely stopped talking long enough to breathe, she could eat at least five times her weight in Big Macs.

As with every question before—half of which he hadn't understood because she either talked too quickly or used words that didn't mean what he thought they did—Elena didn't wait for him to acknowledge her before continuing.

"Are all gargoyles as brain-dead as you, or did my sister just draw the short straw?"

"What?" He turned from the cell door, thinking he'd suffer less pain ramming his head against it than dealing with Emma's sister.

They might look alike, but as far as he could tell, that's where the similarities ended.

"Why didn't you tell Emma the truth before you let Gareth

waltz her right out of the cell?"

"And have her feel even more responsible for what happens to me? She needs to stay focused on the sorcerer, not wonder what's going on down here."

"You do realize if you had told her the truth, she'd at least think twice about sacrificing a future with you. What does she have to lose by accepting Gareth if she believes you'll never feel the same way about her?"

Well, fuck.

"Going by the light-bulb moment you look to be having, I'm going to venture that you didn't think that far ahead, huh?"

He shook his head, a little distracted by what a light bulb had to do with anything.

"Gargoyles." Elena sighed. "Too busy following their damn instincts to stop and think for a minute."

"You accuse me of not thinking things through when you have a fondness for finding trouble."

"So an hour in a cell together and you think you know me now, is that it?"

"Emma certainly seems to."

Elena turned away. "Sometimes my sister sees exactly what she wants to."

"So you don't regularly drag her into trouble?"

"Of course I do. But it's not because I need help." She gestured to her body, her tracings. "I'm quite capable actually."

"So why involve her?"

"It used to be her involving me when we were young. I was the one who had to smooth things over with our father, and then when she vanished for a few days, everything changed. Her magic slowed down while mine continued to grow. I was afraid that if I gave her time to dwell on that, on how little power she had for a sorceress, she'd feel sorry for herself instead of focusing on her strengths. Don't tell Emma I said this, but magic isn't everything."

Vulnerability blinked across her face, so briefly he might have imagined it.

"And I meant what I said earlier," she added. "It's the only fun she has." She eyed their surroundings before adding, "Most of the time. But just for the record, I didn't have anything to do with the Gareth situation."

"Your father," he guessed, assuming Emma hadn't been the one to take steps for an alliance.

Elena nodded. "He's been hard on her, and as much I hated that, I think he was worried she'd end up a victim if he didn't take steps to protect her. Though technically speaking, if you hadn't used these on Emma—" she shook her wrists, "—Urien wouldn't have had a prayer of stopping me from kicking his ass in Vegas."

"Sorry to have inconvenienced you," he drawled. "Give it another hundred years and we'll call it even."

She grinned. "I think you and I will get along just fine, gargoyle."

Something hit the cell door, and they both turned as it swung open.

He recognized the Fae, Amelina, immediately. "What are you doing here?"

"Emma needs you." She approached Elena, and he growled in warning. Both females stared at him.

The Fae rolled her eyes. "She is the one who cursed you, isn't she?"

"She's also my mate's sister." And whether he liked it or not, that meant something.

"I'm sure once she has the cuff off, she'll be fine."

Elena nodded. "I'm good here. Anyone with such fabulous taste in boots can't be all bad."

Amelina grinned at that, then put her hand over the cuff. "Better get a move on, puss."

Lingering only long enough to shift into his cat form, he raced out the door, following Emma's scent. The few men he passed were already unconscious—Amelina's work?—but the one in an upstairs hall, where Emma's scent was the strongest so far, was very much awake.

Urien.

He lunged forward, the power in his front limbs taking the Fae to the floor. He snapped his jaws, finding the Fae's arm instead of his throat, but still tearing through flesh.

The second the scent of the Fae's blood hit his nostrils, he bit down harder, crushing bone.

Urien yelled and kicked him off. Hitting the wall knocked the air from his lungs, but he scrambled right back to his feet. Ready for him this time, Urien vanished before Cian could tackle him a second time, appearing directly behind him.

The sound of Urien's sword being ripped from its scabbard gave Cian all the warning he needed. Low to the ground, he circled the Fae, waiting.

Emma's scent, laced with fear and anger, assailed him, and he snarled, backtracking down the hall, wanting to get closer to his mate.

"Not so brave anymore, gargoyle?" Urien smirked.

Sounds of a struggle drifted from the stairs, but he kept his gaze trained on the Fae. He wouldn't be much good to his mate with a sword stuck in his side. Urien lunged from the right, and at the last second Cian dodged the other way, colliding with the

Fae who had been using a glamour to throw him off.

Taken by surprise, Urien was slow to get his sword up, and Cian slashed with his claws. Cradling his injured arm to his body, Urien took a step back. Cian prowled forward, then stopped, the scent of his enemy suddenly behind him.

Another glamour.

"Don't even think about it."

In front of him, Urien's image faded, and he turned to find the Fae with his arm back, his sword at the ready, but his gaze locked on Amelina.

He dropped the sword without hesitation, sweeping into a bow so low he could have licked the floor. "Your Highness."

'"You will no longer interfere in my family's affairs. Is that understood?"

Urien raised his head, his eyes wide. "I had no idea. Of course. I—"

"If you leave now, I see no reason my mother needs to hear about your treachery."

Urien snapped his good arm across his chest, his fist over his heart. "My loyalty is with Titania. Always."

"I'll be sure to pass that along."

Elena caught up with them just as Urien took off down the hall. She smirked. "Should have known he'd high-tail it out of here the second he knew I was free."

Next to her, the Fae smiled and Cian recognized the family resemblance at once. Wondering if Emma was as oblivious as Elena appeared to be needed to wait until later.

He turned, darting up the stairs in search of his mate.

Emma was still pacing when Gareth strolled into the room. He stopped, seeming puzzled when he saw her father. "Did you need to speak with me, Roan? We can talk outside since Emma needs time to prepare for the ceremony."

"There isn't going to be one."

Gareth sighed. "I realize you may be annoyed by my methods, but no harm has come to either of your daughters, and Elena is perfectly fine."

"This isn't about that."

Gareth's gaze turned hostile. "Don't tell me Emma has confessed to loving the gargoyle, and you are breaking the agreement to indulge her."

Her father only shrugged, offering no explanation. "Agreements have been broken for less."

"Not at such treacherous times. I know you've heard the rumors. The whispers of the gods awakening and another Campaign on the horizon. Maybe even this century. You need all the alliances you can get."

"Not anymore—"

That was all he got out before Gareth struck him down with a burst of pure energy that knocked her father across the room.

"No!"

Emma lunged forward.

Gareth raised his palm but didn't release the energy brewing there. "Where's the dagger, Emma?"

She didn't say anything.

"I know you have it. I pay my oracle well to keep me informed of circumstances I can take advantage of. Where is it?"

"It belongs with Rhiannon."

Gareth scoffed. "Don't tell me you're an Arthur

sympathizer? Avalon didn't stop moving because he died, and there is nothing to be gained by sitting and awaiting a prophecy. Do you really think even the mighty Arthur could prevent another Campaign?" He shook his head as though what she thought ultimately didn't matter.

"If you are so convinced I have the dagger, then take it from me."

He closed his hand, extinguishing the flame, and stalked toward her.

She reached behind her, withdrawing the dagger at her back. She closed her eyes, focusing on the magic inside her, on channeling it, and gripped the hilt.

Nothing.

No power. No strength. Just an ordinary blade.

Gareth slammed her up against the wall, curling his fingers around her throat as he ripped the blade out of her hand. "Did you really think you were strong enough to use it?"

"Use what?"

His eyes narrowed. "The dagger."

"The dagger you think you're holding?" She smiled, knowing this was probably the most important bluff of her life. "You did notice my tracing earlier. The one with the Fae glyphs."

He frowned at her neck.

"Did my father fail to mention I was half Fae when he struck that agreement? And you do know what Fae are best at, right?"

Gareth stared at the dagger.

"Glamours," she continued, though she knew he'd caught on.

He shook his head. "I can feel its power."

She smirked. "You feel what I want you to feel."

The second doubt flashed across his face, she drove her knee up between his legs, then wrenched his wrist back when he curled in on himself, cursing. He dropped the blade, and she kicked it across the floor.

"Bitch," he snarled, backhanding her.

The force behind the blow knocked her to the floor. Blood pooled across her tongue.

She raised her head just as Cian launched himself through the open door, tackling Gareth. He had the sorcerer pinned before Emma could snap her head around to follow the movement, but Gareth recovered quickly.

The chair she'd been sitting on earlier shattered from the impact of Gareth's fireball, the blast knocking Cian across the room.

Digging her feet in, Emma dove across the floor, her fingers closing around the dagger. Gareth staggered upright, gaze locked on her. Cian growled, but instead of lunging for the sorcerer, he backed up until he was by her side. He nudged her with his head.

"I suppose that's no more than a twig?"

She smiled sweetly at Gareth. "You mean the dagger I lied about?"

His expression turned homicidal, and she read his intentions a heartbeat before he struck. The hilt of the dagger glowed purple, and fire raced across her palm and up her arm until she cried out. Power slammed through her, literally knocking her off her feet.

Holy shit.

She couldn't breathe, couldn't move—and when she opened her eyes and discovered the four-hundred-pound cat smothering her, she knew why.

Cian prodded her cheek, his whiskers tickling her skin.

"I'm okay."

After another nuzzle, the sound in his chest was less of a growl and more of a purr. She raised her head, scanning the room for Gareth and finding only her father and…a fluffy white bunny?

She glanced at the dagger. Seriously? The one Elena used had turned Cian to stone, and she'd reduced Gareth to a fuzzy, pink-eyed herbivore? *Seriously?*

Cian finally gave her some breathing room, pausing to lick her first. She laughed and ran her hand over his head before sitting up.

"Ew." Elena crossed the room with Leah right on her heels. She took the rabbit from their father. "Em, that was totally badass, minus Peter Cottontail here."

"She's still working out the kinks." Leah smiled and pulled her to her feet, almost tripping over Cian, who stuck right to Emma's side. "Told you." She pulled her into a fierce hug.

Elena glanced at her father, who hadn't stopped glaring at Cian in a serious I-eat- gargoyles-who-hurt-my-daughter-for-breakfast way that only a father could pull off.

"I missed something big, didn't I?"

"Colossal actually."

She cocked her head, her gaze landing on Leah's boots. "That's weird. My boots have almost the same mark on them from this wolf who was looking to nail my friend."

Their father made a choking sound. "Wolf?"

Elena continued to stare at the boots. "He struck out anyway since she's still hung up on some old flame."

Oh boy.

Leah's face flushed pink, and she snatched Gareth out of Elena's arms. "I'll take care of him." She bolted out the door.

"What's her deal?" Elena sighed, then arched a brow at their father. "Were you just staring at her ass?"

Cian snorted, butting his head against Emma.

"I guess I should tell her, huh?"

"Tell who what?" Elena linked her arm through Emma's. "You know, I think I hear a blackjack table calling my name. I wonder if Leah's free."

She watched their father dart into the hall. "I think she's got her hands full with an old flame, actually."

Three weeks later

Emma clicked off the remote and stuffed it down the side of the couch. "We're done."

"Come on, Em." Cian hovered over her, using his leg to keep her trapped beneath him.

"It's been almost six hours. I can't take any more." She wiggled out from under him, which was really more of an awkward slide to the floor.

He leaned down, his nose bumping hers. "Please?"

"If I watch any more Looney Tunes today, I'll be dreaming of dropping anvils on your head."

"Ouch." He spanned his fingers across her jaw. "We can't have that."

She closed her eyes, her heart picking up speed even though she knew she had to get up. They'd never make it to the bedroom if they got started here, and the last thing she wanted was one of Cian's siblings walking in on them.

With the exception of Briana, they had the place mostly to themselves. Cale and Sorcha never stayed for long when they did return, and Tristan and Kennedy spent the majority of their time at Pendragon's or in Avalon.

She and Cian had actually planned on heading to Avalon themselves, but when Cian had found the Looney Toons marathon on television, he'd been quick to suggest waiting another day or two. He was either avoiding her sister, who talked non-stop about the Fae court since discovering their truth about Leah and being royalty, or her father.

Assuming it was the latter, she'd caved. Although her father was so preoccupied with picking arguments with Leah whenever their paths crossed—which seemed to be a lot these days, thanks to Elena—she doubted he'd be up for giving Cian a hard time anyway.

"You know what we could have, though? Food."

"That's not exactly the appetite I was hoping to appease at the moment, but if food is what you truly crave—" he opened his mouth over hers, "—then who am I to deny you?"

"Mmmm," was about the only response she could put together when he was done kissing the life out of her. She leaned away from that sensational mouth of his before it was responsible for getting her naked.

He sighed. "I guess that means I'm cooking."

"Assuming you don't want burnt food." Once set of scorch marks on the ceiling was enough to live down, and that was after they'd only been back two days.

"I still don't understand how you can burn—"

She slapped her hand over his mouth. "Keep talking and it won't just be in my dreams when I start dropping anvils."

Cian laughed and hauled her up, holding her against him.

Leaning into him, she whispered, “Close your eyes.” And the second he did, she shoved him backward and darted around the couch, heading for the door.

She heard his feet hit the floor behind her, imagined he’d hopped right over the couch to pursue her. He could have caught her in the hall and they both knew it. Instead, he waited until she skidded around the corner and into the kitchen before he pounced.

She pivoted and dropped into a crouch, making herself as small a target as possible, the way Sorcha had shown her. Less than two feet away, Cian stopped, but his gaze was locked on something else.

The patio door opened, and Briana stepped inside. Her posture mirrored Cian’s when she noticed them in the room. The tension in the room jumped a hundred degrees, and Emma glanced between the two.

Then she glanced outside and saw the sun had risen, and instead of playing gargoyle on the roof, Briana looked like she’d just been caught unwrapping all her Christmas presents while everyone else was asleep.

“How… When… Who…” Cian stopped. “Who?” he repeated.

Emma rolled her eyes, grateful she’d never had any protective older brothers. She’d bet Cian was grateful for that to.

Too bad that didn’t stop him from crossing his arms. “Why didn’t you tell me?”

His sister only shrugged, leaving Emma to fill in the silence. “Why not just shove her under a bright light? We can even play good cop, bad cop.”

Cian scowled at her, and Briana tried to take advantage of the distraction to retreat back the way she’d come without saying a word.

"Briana."

"Not now, Cian." She growled and shoved past him when he tried to get between her and the door.

Cian stared after her, and Emma joined him in time to see Briana's sleek cat form disappear into the trees.

She slid her arms around his waist, snuggling up against his back. "She'll be okay."

He shook his head. "She's been hiding it, hasn't she? Why?"

"Maybe she's not ready to share who her mate is."

"Do you know something?" He glanced over his shoulder at her.

"Even if I did, it would be Briana's story to tell." And all she really had at the moment were some strong suspicions about a particular wraith.

"That's not answering the question."

She slipped around him and closed the door before taking his hand. "A very wise man once told me that it's best not to get between siblings."

He snorted. "I said that once, and I'm pretty sure Elena had threatened to sew my tail to my balls at the time."

Leading him out of the kitchen, Emma headed for their bedroom, intent on distracting him. She didn't have to try very hard. Once they were through the door, he slammed it closed and whirled to pin her against it.

"Bed," she whispered, loving the way his hands slid right under her top, boldly cupping her breasts.

"Why?" He bent his head, running his mouth down her throat.

She moaned, raking at his shoulders. "Because."

"Because you'll be closer to the restraints you stashed under the bed earlier?"

"You know about them?" She pushed at his chest.

"Did you think I subjected myself to hours of Elmer Fudd and Daffy Duck for the sheer enjoyment of it? I've been waiting all night for you to dig them out."

Suspicious, she searched his eyes. "Really? I hadn't expected you to be so receptive."

"To being chained up so you can have your wicked way with me?"

"Well, when you put it like that..."

He laughed and slanted his mouth across hers for a hard, feverish kiss that left her trembling inside. She had only a second to get her brain back online, and then he dragged her into the bedroom.

Grinning, he dropped onto the edge of the bed and held up his hands.

He was making it all too easy. She'd expected it to take some convincing. "What are you up to?"

"Me? You're the one with the handcuffs stashed under the bed."

"How did you even spot them, anyway?" She bent over to grab them, not even making it halfway before he scooped her up and tossed her on the bed.

He grinned down at her, his body pressing her into the mattress.

"You never had any intention of submitting to me, did you?"

"I've already surrendered my heart. Or isn't that enough?"

Heart pounding from that intense look in his eyes, she pretended to mull it over. "Nope."

He nipped her shoulder. "You're determined to have all of me, are you?"

Locking her arms around his neck, she drew him closer. "Don't I have you now?"

He slowly swept his mouth across hers. "Until the day I die."

About the Author

A born and raised Maritimer, Sydney Somers fell in love with writing at the age of eight. Since finishing her first book in 2002, Sydney has written over twenty-five romances—one of which will forever remain hidden under her bed.

When she's not tracking down remote controls, chasing after three very energetic children or exterminating rogue dust bunnies, Sydney can be found curled up with a good book or working on her next sexy, paranormal romance. She loves to hear from readers and invites them to e-mail her (sydney@sydneysomers.com) or drop by her website (www.sydneysomers.com) any time.

Scorching desire...fatal consequences.

Dark Obsession

© 2010 Sydney Somers

Shadow Destroyers, Book 4

Demon slayer Rae McAvoy refuses to let anything stand between her and getting the job done. Especially her ex. Loving Parker nearly destroyed her, and if partnering with him one last time means he'll be reassigned and out of her life for good, bring it on.

If Parker was the only threat to her heart, tracking down one rogue scientist would be a snap. Except the scientist in question is Rae's father, and his experiments are hitting much too close to home.

Parker Walsh hasn't forgotten the passion that once burned between them, and he's determined to remind Rae every chance he gets. But giving in to more than just lust could mean surrendering to the darkness inside him—the same darkness that once drove her away.

Riding the edge of their rising desire pushes them to the breaking point, until an explosion of passion raises the stakes even higher. Especially when long-buried secrets force them to break the last links to their past—or else be consumed by an obsession so dark it could tear them apart for good.

Warning: Contains a fierce battle of wills between reunited lovers, explosive sexual tension, sarcasm, gritty demon-slaying violence, scorching sex and a love worth fighting for.

CPSIA information can be obtained at www.ICGtesting.com
Printed in the USA
267147BV00001B/2/P

9 781609 282998